THE FIGURE OF A
MAN FROLICKED
WITH THE GRA
DOLPHIN.



"He appears to be perfectly adapted to aquatic life, displaying great agility and strength," Elizabeth Merrill reported to Lt. Ainsley and Admiral Pierce. "The chest cavity is water-filled with gills in place of normal lung tissue. Skin appears humanoid with dolphin-like characteristics. His feet are webbed, his eyes are catlike in action, able to see at ocean depths in almost total darkness. He has not spoken, though he's got vocal equipment. I have the impression he understands a good deal. As for his origins, he's given us very little to go on. We took every scrap of information we had and fed it to Big Daddy at the Defense Department and the computer sent back an answer."

The three of them looked up at the monitor as the computer ran its incredible printout:

**LAST CITIZEN OF ATLANTIS???**

#1

# MAN FROM ATLANTIS

Richard Woodley

A DELL BOOK

Published by
Dell Publishing Co., Inc.
1 Dag Hammarskjold Plaza
New York, New York 10017



ISBN: 0-440-15368-9

Printed in the United States of America
First printing—October 1977
Second printing—November 1977

## chapter 1

It was a rare storm, one that puzzled the meteorologists. Lacking the familiar configurations of a hurricane or typhoon, it formed suddenly from the confluence of several smaller storms hundreds of miles at sea, far to the west of the coast of California. The mingling of errant gales wildly churned the depths of the Pacific.

Radio messages from freighters and large fishing boats reported fifty-foot waves, and winds and temperatures that rose and fell with horrendous inconsistency. Weathermen at widely separated shore stations frantically compared notes, trying both to fathom the eerie flukiness and to prepare themselves for the arrival of the storm on shore.

In the end there were no valid or useful predictions. The separate storms met and mixed quickly to form the vast, crazy weather pattern, the winds and rains swirled over the Pacific in ominous magnificence for a couple of hours, and then it was over. The storm never really arrived at the coast.

While tides and waves were higher than usual along the shore, there was none of the threatened destruction of beach homes and marinas. Still, the storm at sea had been awesome. Meteorologists would be able to reflect on the phenomenon for weeks, develop, advance, and discard their theories over hundreds of radio and TV broadcasts. They would talk of ice ages and droughts and rearrangements of the earth's fertile zones.

For even though the destructive force of the storm never reached land, it was without precedent in their loose-leaf histories of weather. And the reputations of weathermen would be enhanced not by writing the storm off as a fluke of nature, but by expounding grand notions and humble warnings about the wondrous powers of climate and how little we really knew about the intricate workings of our natural world.

In the immediate aftermath of the mighty storm's near brush with land, the waves beat on the shore, boiling up kelp and fish and debris and hurling it all high onto the sand. Lightning pierced the night sky. Gusts of wind alternated with moments of stark calm. Shore birds sought lee inland.

The beach was deserted except for a man and boy walking along the spindrift fringes of the waves, poking at the debris with walking sticks. Their Dalmatian pranced on ahead, sniffing here and there at pieces of wood and seaweed, and barking at an occasional fish or small shark left gasping on the sand.

"Hey Dad," the boy called, "look at this!" Lightning flashes illuminated the remains of a small wrecked boat with Japanese letters on its wooden planks. The man came over and poked at the planks with his stick. "Suppose anybody was aboard, Dad?"

"Not lately, Wyatt. The wood is rotting. It was probably sunk out there for a long time before the storm brought it up."

"I'm sorry we didn't get the whole storm here. That would have been exciting."

"It would have been exciting, all right. But it would have caused a lot of damage, from what they say. We sure could have used the rain, though. They're already rationing water up north, in the San Francisco area."

"Because of the drought."

"Right."

They walked on together, jabbing their gnarled sticks into the wet sand, feeling the wind tousling their hair. The man's thinning hair was gray, his face weather-beaten.

"Dad, how come there's so many different seaweeds and stuff that I've never seen on the beach before?"

"I guess it's because the storm was so powerful. Usually it doesn't disturb the bottom out there much. But in this case it looks like it churned up a whole lot of things that probably hadn't been bothered in ages, stuff that just lay on the bottom of the sea. Quite a blow, all right."

"What would it have been like, on a boat?"

"Scary. Really scary."

"Even on a big boat?"

"You bet."

"What can you do, if you're on a boat out there in a storm like that?"

"Hold her bow into the wind, if possible. And keep some power under you."

"That's all?"

"And pray. That's about all you can do. Good ship, good man at the helm, and a good man upstairs watching over you can bring you through most blows."

Their dog stopped to paw at a large clump of kelp.

Suddenly it stepped back and growled. It darted in and out toward the pile, barking excitedly. A wave washed in over the clump, and the dog scooted back out of the way. Then it advanced quickly in the path of the retreating wave and growled viciously.

"Take it easy, Measles!" the boy called. "It's okay!"

They continued walking casually toward the clump of seaweed. The dog yipped persistently, dancing around, thrusting its nose close to the pile, scratching around the edges of it. The lip of another wave washed over, but this time the dog did not retreat. It remained next to the pile, scratching with its front paws.

"Some darned dying sand shark is gonna snap his nose off one day," the man said.

They ambled up to the seaweed and Wyatt pushed the dog away and ran with him further up the beach.

The man stood looking at the seaweed. A bolt of lightning lit the scene, and wind fluttered his shirt. He prodded at the kelp with his stick. It hit something solid. As he knelt beside the clump to investigate it, a wave washed over his bare feet. Lightning flashed again and again.

And then the man saw what was enmeshed in the seaweed, what had excited the dog. His mouth dropped open, his eyes widened. It was a human hand, nearly black, its fingers curled like talons and moving slightly.

He leaned forward and gently pulled away some of the seaweed. Under it was a man, kelp tightly wound around his muscled body. He was clad only in skin-tight trunks. Rumbles of distant thunder paused long enough for Wyatt's father to hear the man's faint, tortured gasps.

The man struggled weakly in the sand, reaching with one blackened hand, clawing at the seaweed with the other.

"Oh my God." With greater urgency, Wyatt's father pulled away more of the seaweed and was about to cradle the man's head in his arm when he thought better of it. Not knowing the extent of the man's injuries, he dared not move him at all.

He sprang to his feet. "Wyatt!" He tried to keep his voice calm. "Come here right away!"

Wyatt trotted back with the dog. The dog immediately approached the seaweed where the man lay half-buried, and began to growl again.

"Wyatt, run home, call the police. Tell them we need an ambulance. There's a man hurt here."

"What?"

"Just do what I say, Wyatt. Run on home. Hurry. If you're fast enough, you may help save this man's life."

"Can I just see what . . ."

"Go! The man is *dying*, Wyatt!"

It was an old house elegantly remodeled, with a giant bay window overlooking the sea like a ship's bridge. A party honoring the retired captain's anniversary was in progress there. Navy men were in dress blues, civilians wore dark, formal suits and long gowns. For the most part, the party had confined itself inside in deference to the expected storm, but now a couple of the guests were out in the backyard garden, enjoying the cool breeze and the pleasant, distant thunder, or wandering over to the edge of the cliff for a glimpse of the wind-tossed Pacific. Tall torches were placed around the garden, their oil-fed flames flickering in the wind.

Near a tall and bushy forsythia, a man and woman stood close together, talking softly.

"Hey there, behind the bushes," came a woman's voice from the patio, "do I see some friendlies?"

The man and woman turned. The man was wearing a black dinner suit and black bow tie, the woman was dressed in a chic pastel-green chiffon gown topped with a diaphanous trailing wrap.

The woman who called was the hostess, the captain's wife. She wore a fluffy blue evening dress and her graying hair was neatly coiffed. She smiled at the couple. "Doug and Elizabeth, are you friendlies?"

"We're friendlies," Elizabeth Merrill answered cheerfully, tossing her long, blond hair.

"Friendly as can be," said Doug Berkeley, turning toward the captain's wife and smiling.

She lifted the hem of her long gown and came carefully down the steps and walked over to them. "Well then," she glanced behind her and then took one of their elbows in each of her hands, "come inside and get the party started." She leaned between them and added conspiratorially, "We need some lively young people to get things moving."

"I thought things were already moving an hour ago," Doug said.

"Oh, you know how Navy people are," she said, smoothing her gown. "They're all dears, so proper and obedient and stiff. They all stand around, sipping when the captain sips, smiling when the captain smiles, answering when the captain speaks. Navy all the way. It's as if they can never let down, so long as they're in uniform. Come," she turned and started toward the house, "we need a healthy dose of young, beautiful people out of uniform. You'll remind them that they're all human beings, underneath those dress blues. I wouldn't have interrupted you for less."

"You didn't interrupt anything," Elizabeth said brightly, starting after her. "Doug was giving me brotherly advice."

"Aw . . ." he winced and caught up with Elizabeth.

The woman disappeared into the house.

"You can't really think of me as a brother," Doug said softly as they walked up the steps to the patio.

"I don't—really." She smiled at him.

"Well then, why . . ."

"Sorry this is such a bore."

"I like service parties." He squared his shoulders.

"I don't. If I'm not working in the lab, I'd rather be diving. I get withdrawal symptoms if I'm out of the water too long."

They moved across the patio.

"Can that be your only hobby, Liz?"

"What else is there? You only call me Liz when you're annoyed."

He chuckled and tried to draw her to him, but she gracefully eluded his arm. "Duty calls." She smiled and opened the door for him.

Doug shook his head and scratched his ear. "Sometimes I think you're only attracted to fish."

"Whatever else you many think," she took his elbow and guided him through the door, "I've never seen a fish quite as handsome as you, not yet. Although I haven't been below a hundred feet in quite a while."

• • •

White-coated interns and nurses bustled around the small emergency room. A young resident physician swept the curtain aside and stepped in. "What's up?"

He went quickly to the side of the cardio-pulmonary-resuscitation table where the man from the beach lay, covered with a white sheet from his shoulders to his feet. His face was blue. His breath came in hoarse gasps. A breathing bag was attached to a tube that entered his mouth. The corps of interns and nurses stared in frustration and worry.

"Found him on the beach, unconscious and barely alive," said one intern, rubbing his chin. "Drowning maybe, but . . ."

"We got him tubed and bagged with a hundred-percent oxygen," said a nurse in a nervous, quaking voice. "Trying to get him ventilated. BP is palpable at seventy. Pulse one-fifty and thready. We don't know if—"

"He really looks cyanotic," said the resident, elbowing between the others to bend over the man. "Well, let's get a couple of lines going. CVP in the central line—"

"I need a sixteen-gauge short intro cath," the intern said as he turned quickly to a nurse.

"And I want a peripheral line with two amps of dopamine in 500 of D-5," the resident touched the man's cheek with the back of his hand, "and start the drip at thirty a minute. That ought to bring him up. And let's get a portable chest and get the EKG tech in here. What are those stirrups doing in here? We need more room."

"Delivery room was full," a nurse said, "we had to bring one in here."

"Well, get that table out. Jesus Christ. People

should have babies at home. Back to nature. If this guy was gonna go swimming in that storm, he should have used the buddy system. When we bring him around, I think I'll send him back to summer camp for a refresher course. John," he turned to the intern, "was there any vomiting? Blood? Did you pump him out?"

"He had some water in him, Doctor, but he's clear now. I checked the tube. No obstructions, no broken teeth. I did get some head trauma. Looks like he got bopped with something."

"Yeah, maybe a submarine. That old beachcomber Burger found him? I thought he only picked up rotten wood and dead sharks."

"This time he found us a live one, Doctor." The intern looked at the resident for a responding smile, but he didn't get one.

"Did you check the guy's eyes? He could have O.D.'d on something good."

The intern bent over the man and lifted an eyelid with his thumb.

"Better give me a liter of saline and open it wide." The resident prowled around the table, checking the tubes.

The head nurse was on the phone. "We need a stat EKG and a stat portable chest X-ray—"

"And a skull set," the resident put in.

"—and a set of skull film."

"How are his eyes?" The resident looked back over his shoulder while he arranged some silver tools on a tray. "They constricted? Dilated? What?"

"Well, they're unh, at midpoint," the intern said.

"Okay. Listen, nurse." The nearest nurse, with her hands clasped over her stomach, looked quickly up at him. "Let's push, oh, point two NARCAN just to be on the safe side."

"But they're funny."

"Hunh?" The resident turned back to the table, where the intern had both the man's eyes propped open with his thumbs.

"The eyes are funny."

The resident bent down. "Funny is not exactly a clinical description, but I see what you mean."

The man's eyes held open by the intern were wide and staring. They were an almost solid green, with small points of white in the centers.

Another intern prepared to put in the first intravenous line. He reached under the sheet and exposed the man's limp arm. "Hey, what's this?" He gaped at the blackened hand. "Why's it like that?"

The resident shook his head. "Let's just concentrate on getting him breathing first."

The man gasped weakly for breath, his chest barely moving. His face was a deathly gray-blue, like slate. Interns and nurses attached the various tubes to his arms and neck, and positioned the hanging bottles above him. The X-ray technician and two assistants wheeled in their gear and positioned the X-ray machine over him.

The technician adjusted the plate under his body. "Okay," she said, backing off with the remote switch in her hand, "I'm shooting."

A whir came from behind the dark cone of the machine as the motor revved up.

"Hurry up with that film, will you?" the resident said, pacing back and forth. "I know you guys prefer to send it out to Kodak, but this guy may have just a few minutes left."

The X-ray technician scowled at the jibe and took another shot. "We're doing the best we can, Doctor."

"Yeah, right. Move it."

The technician scurried out with her photographic plates.

"What do you think, Doctor?" one of the interns asked, clasping his hands behind him to emulate the resident.

"What do I think? I think the guy needs a vacation in the Sahara. What should I think?"

The intern reddened. "I just meant, he seems a little strange."

"Yeah, well, let's just save our curiosity for later, when we've kept him from becoming a little dead, if you know what I mean."

The captain stood in a corner of the room, surrounded by nodding junior officers.

Several of the guests clustered around a buffet table, sipping at colorful, fruity drinks.

"Well, gentlemen," Elizabeth said, smiling at two Navy men sitting straight-backed on the sofa, right legs crossed over left, hands clasped over knees, "how are things on the bounding main?"

"Well, things are just fine, Dr. Merrill," said one, nodding.

"Shipshape would you say?"

"Yes, ma'am," the young officer smiled, "you might say."

"Cutbacks being felt yet?" Doug Berkeley asked.

"Well, you know," the other officer said, watching his foot bounce in the air, "whatever the President says, we can live with."

"Including having women serve on board ships?"

"Well, yes, sure. Haven't seen any yet, out our way. But, you know, the Navy is used to doing whatever's required. My own view," he glanced around the room, then continued quietly, "is that women won't be, unh, particularly happy on ships. But if that's what's . . ."

"If you can't lick em," Elizabeth saw the officer blush, "join em."

"Yes, ma'am."

"Lot of changes in the Navy," Doug offered, "what with beards and so forth, right?"

"Well, we pride ourselves on being up to date," the first officer said. "We change with the times."

"You guys ever relax?" Elizabeth smiled at them.

"Oh, yes ma'am," the officer nodded and smiled back, "but I see what you mean. As far as the two of us are concerned, you know, this is our first time in the captain's house. And we're pretty junior, you know."

"I understand." Her eyes showed that she did. "How's your dolphin work coming?"

"Oh, it's real good." The second officer brightened. "We got a little bad flack, you know, after Vietnam. Rumors about them carrying bombs strapped on their backs and so forth. But I really love those things. They become like friends. They're as smart as we are, you know. Once we crack their speech patterns, we'll really have something going."

"Or once they crack ours."

"That's a fact."

"Maybe they already have," Doug said.

"Maybe, Doctor." The officer chuckled and shook his head. "Boy, I'll tell you, sometimes you could almost believe they have, the way they respond to you."

"The thing I like about them," Elizabeth said, "is

that they seem to have no hostility at all, except when they have to defend themselves or each other, or their human friends."

"That's true, Dr. Merrill. They're friendly nearly all the time."

"Maybe we could learn something from that," Doug said.

"I know what you mean, Dr. Berkeley," the first officer said. "But the trouble with that is, friendly as you and I would like to be with the world, there are too many human beings who just aren't all that friendly. All dolphins are friendly, you know what I mean? They don't have to worry about one group of dolphins trying to take over another."

"That's what makes human beings so specially delightful," Elizabeth said. "Somebody's always trying to hurt somebody else. Dolphins have apparently discovered that peace is fun enough."

"Well, not at any price, ma'am, is my view on peace. I agree with you that dolphins are real nice and all, and they seem to have a lot of fun. But for all that, I'd still rather be a human than a dolphin."

"Dr. Berkeley?" The captain's wife strode briskly over to the coffee table.

"Yes?"

"Telephone. You can take it right through there, on your left."

"Okay. Thanks." He handed Elizabeth his drink. "Keep it lively, kid," he said softly.

She grinned and watched him disappear into the next room.

"If you'll excuse us, Dr. Merrill," the first officer got up and bowed slightly, then the second did the same, "we're supposed to circulate."

"Of course. I should probably be doing the same. See you later."

Phil Roth, a young, dark-haired man with broad shoulders, in the uniform of a lieutenant commander with several service stripes on the chest, came up behind the sofa and leaned over beside Elizabeth. "How are all the frogs and dogs?"

"Oh, hi, Phil. I got promoted to dolphins."

"Any closer to getting your own research operation?"

"Who knows? I doubt it. Research money is tight like everything else these days. And there are still people who question the abilities of the woman-as-scientist-administrator type. Especially money people. They figure women researchers are fine, as long as they've got some stable male to supervise them and keep them from breaking into tears all the time. How about you?"

"Couple new things. Want to get out of here?"

"Can't. Occupied."

"Oh? Doesn't look to me like you're so—"

"How are you, Phil?" She put her arm along the sofa back and touched his hand.

He stared at her for a few seconds, half smiling. "I'm fine."

"You look good."

He cocked his head and narrowed his eyes. It was a typical comment from Elizabeth, a compliment he didn't know quite how to take. He supposed it was a simple observation, friendly, nothing more. "The Navy keeps me healthy. Diving and so forth. I've got a new assignment that I'm pretty excited about."

She waited for him to continue, but he looked away casually. "So tell me."

"I'm not supposed to talk a whole lot about it."

"You know me. I'm a clam."

"Yeah." In fact, she was. She was a listener, a brain, a counselor, a friend, and, when it came to security, a clam. You could tell her anything or ask her anything, about any subject, and whether she liked what you said or not, she kept it between the two of you. That was, for Phil, one of her most enchanting qualities. One of them. The other main one was that she was so very attractive, a truly beautiful woman, tall, lean, shapely, with sloping dark blue eyes. And she managed to keep an air of mystery about her, which he liked too. Or if he didn't exactly like it, it made her even more attractive. "I'm going to command the *Sea Quest* on her next dive."

"Hey, really?" She grinned and clasped his hand. "That's terrific! I'm proud of you. Also I envy you. Where're you taking her?"

"Well," he studied his hands, "I'm really not supposed to say . . ."

"If it bothers you, don't. We'll know about it soon enough. That's really exciting, Phil . . ."

Dr. Berkeley leaned against the wall and turned his head toward it, holding the phone tight to his ear. "Wait a minute, wait a minute, slow down. So far what I understand is you found this guy on the beach; you brought him back, you tubed him up, you took pictures. Now, take it from there . . . What? . . . It shows what? Slow down . . . Oh come on . . ."

He closed his eyes and nodded as he listened. "I see. And Dr. Bock's in charge? Well, he knows what he's doing . . ." Jordan Bock knew what he was doing, all right. He was as skillful and clever as any resident he'd ever seen. The only trouble with Dr. Bock was, he was too damn young and too damn smart. But in any event, he knew what he was doing, and if Bock wanted him called, it meant something. "Yeah, sure. Be there in a few minutes."

Phil came around the sofa and sat down next to Elizabeth. "So I was pretty discouraged for a while, and thought about getting out and hitching up with some private outfit—maybe even salvage. But you know how it is with private outfits, never any money and so forth. So this opportunity came along, and I started to do a lot of thinking about the Navy and the budget and what I'd really like to accomplish—crazy dreams like that . . ."

"Elizabeth." Doug walked quickly over. "Sorry, Elizabeth," he glanced at Phil, "but I have an emergency. Man seems to have forgotten how to breathe. Can I put you in a cab, or . . ." He glanced again at Phil.

"Forgotten how to breathe?" Elizabeth leaned forward.

"Something like that. You interested?"

"Mind if I tag along?"

"Let's go." He turned and started moving away.

Phil took Elizabeth's arm. "Elizabeth, can I talk to you first?"

"Phil, we're sort of rushed . . ." She put her drink down on the coffee table.

"Just for a minute?"

She eased out of his grasp, patted his hand, and stood up. "I'm really sorry, Phil, but there's an emergency, like the doctor said. I'd like to talk to you. We'll do it soon, okay? And would you make our excuses to the captain?" She squeezed his hand.

He looked at her for a moment. Then he returned the squeeze, nodded, released her hand, and stood up beside her. "Okay, sure."

"I'm really sorry."

"Don't be. It's okay. I understand."

She smiled and turned away, then turned back. "Oh, by the way, congratulations, Phil. Really."

"Thanks." He watched her walk away, then moved over to join the crowd around the host.

Elizabeth caught up with Doug at the front door, and they left together. They got into his Monte Carlo and headed for the hospital.

For a while neither of them spoke.

"Who was that back there?" Doug asked finally.

"Back where?"

"At the party, the guy you were talking to."

"Oh, Phil Roth. Old friend. He just got the command of the *Sea Quest,* the Navy's new super research submersible. I guess he wanted to talk about it. You, by the way, are the only person I tell such things to, so you will *not* talk about it."

"Of course not. But I can see why he wants to. It sounds interesting. And dangerous."

"True on both counts, although he'd minimize the danger. He figures the Navy always knows what it's doing, more or less."

"Don't you?"

"More or less. The nice thing about the Navy is, they can afford to do things like that, things you couldn't afford to do on the outside. Of course, it's still the Navy."

"Meaning what?"

"Meaning that the bottom line is always warfare."

"Or defense."

"Okay. Military, then, however you see it."

"Well, you're part of it, though I must admit you don't always sound like you are."

"I'm first a scientist. It's a good deal for me. I'm not complaining."

"But you want out."

"Since when? If I wanted out I'd get out. I just want to run my own research show someday—preferably not connected with the military. But I'm not impatient."

"What a lady."

"What a chauvinist remark." She chuckled.

So did he. "I get confused about that. I never know when I'm complimenting you or when I'm setting myself up to get slapped with an equality poster."

"You're not bad. All men are confused. What was chauvinist about the remark was the fact that if a guy said he'd like to run his own business someday, you would think it was entirely natural and normal. Let's get inside."

In the emergency room, Dr. Bock, the resident, led them over to the view box and turned on the light behind it. He aligned the X-ray photos on the viewer. "You're not going to believe this," he said, glancing up at Elizabeth and Doug.

They leaned to peer over Dr. Bock's shoulders at the X rays. Dr. Bock looked briefly at Elizabeth. "Are you staff, Doctor?"

"Navy."

Doug rubbed his chin and straightened up, still peering at the X rays. "They can't take a decent portable chest, can they?" He reached around and switched off the light. "You better order another set."

"I did," Dr. Bock said, showing no expression. "You're looking at them."

Doug winced. Of course. Bock would have had the same doubts, and would have already made the double check. Doug switched the light on again and leaned close to the pictures, tracing his index finger over the strange, gray shapes in the X rays.

Rather than normal lungs, what they saw in the pictures appeared to be layers of feathery tissue, membranes with no discernible lobes or outer walls.

Doug shook his head. "This guy's had it, I'm afraid. Nearly complete deterioration. No capacity at all. The question is, how did he walk around on the streets with lungs like that? Must have been something eating away inside the tissues for a long time, and then the whole thing just suddenly collapsed into sections. I'm amazed he's still alive."

Elizabeth turned from the pictures and walked over to the bed and stared down at the stricken man. He was trussed up like a turkey. To various spots on his body were connected catheters, intravenous tubes, hanging bottles, monitors. His legs were tightly wrapped in white bandages. His face was blue and dry. His breath came in hoarse and bubbly gasps, growing weaker as she watched. He was comatose, obviously dying. His one free hand moved slightly, his fingers extended as if reaching for something.

She studied his black hand and dark face, the skin of both showing tiny cracks from dehydration.

Two nurses stood quietly beside her, shaking their heads in concern.

The hot overhead lights beat down on the nearly lifeless form.

"Why isn't he sweating?" Elizabeth asked softly.

Doug leaned over beside her. "I don't think that's going to make too much difference. Not now."

"Can you get a skin biopsy?"

"We'd have to move him to County," Dr. Bock said, moving around to the other side of the table.

"There's clearly no time for that," Doug said. "Elizabeth, I'm afraid no one can offer much to someone with desiccated lungs like that."

"If that's what they are."

Doug looked at her, startled. "I beg your pardon."

"He's alive, and by all accounts and evidence he shouldn't be. But he is. Even with his chest like that." She looked across the bed at Dr. Bock. "Was he by any chance found anywhere near the ocean?"

"Yes, as a matter of fact," he said evenly. "Right at the edge of the surf."

"Doug, I'd like to bronch him."

"Now, Liz," he smiled slightly, "wouldn't you rather just go back to the party?"

She straightened her shoulders and looked at him stonily. "I want this guy bronched, Doug. I want to bronch him myself. Right now."

Doug blinked, then nodded to Dr. Bock.

"Bronchoscope," Bock said to the nurses.

In moments the equipment was gathered and arranged. The bronchoscope tube was passed down the man's trachea into his bronchial tubes.

Elizabeth stared closely at the images transmitted on the scope, and commented on what she saw as the tube was worked farther and farther down. A nurse took notes. ". . . I'm looking into the base of the left bronchial branch . . . getting down to the lung stem . . . Now I can see . . ."

She stopped. Her eyes narrowed. Her cheeks flushed.

"Elizabeth?" Doug put a hand on her back, felt its tenseness. "What is it, Elizabeth?"

"Get an ambulance around here."

"But what is it?"

"Taking him to County?" Dr. Bock asked, signaling to a nurse who stepped to the phone.

"No."

"But what is it, Liz? What in blazes do you see?"

She carefully withdrew the bronchoscope from the man's throat. "If I told you, you wouldn't believe it. Just get the ambulance."

"Done," Dr. Bock said.

"Look, Liz, if you have a theory . . ."

"The man is dying. I know how to save him. I think." She whirled around to the nearest nurse. "Turn those lights off. Get the tubes out of him. All of them."

Dr. Bock came quickly around the table and stood face to face with her. "We can't just blindly release him to you."

Elizabeth was breathing hard. "It's twelve feet to that door. Either you're going to help me get him out of here or I'm going to do it myself."

"But Doctor, we can't just let him go, without knowing what you—"

"There's no time for discussion. I'm taking him!"

Bock looked at Doug. Doug looked at Elizabeth. Elizabeth looked down at the man whose breathing was a faint rasp.

"Okay, Dr. Bock," Doug said. "You heard the lady."

"We both did."

"Right. Okay. I'll take responsibility. Let's move."

The wail of the ambulance deepened quickly, then abruptly stopped as it backed up to the emergency-room doors.

The two attendants pulled out the collapsible ambulance litter, rolled it over to the table, raised it to the same height, and stepped back while the doctors carefully moved the man onto the litter and buckled the straps around him.

They wheeled it over to the ambulance and pushed it in. Elizabeth and Doug climbed in after it. The attendants scampered around and slid into the front seat.

The driver looked at Doug in the rear-view mirror. "Sir, where we goin'?"

"Ask her."

" 'Scuse me. Ma'am, where we goin'?"

Elizabeth picked up the man's dark wrist gently, felt for pulse, and checked her watch. "Fastest way to the ocean."

"Ocean?"

"Right," Doug snapped. "Let's roll!"

"Okay." The driver shrugged. He wound the ambulance out through the parking lot onto the street and hit the siren. "Uh, 'scuse me, but any particular place at the ocean?"

"Just the closest place where we can get to the water," Elizabeth said, still holding the man's wrist and looking at her watch.

"That'd be ole Burger's beach." The driver nodded and pushed down on the accelerator, not easing off even to make a sharp left turn.

The other attendant leaned over to the driver and

said quietly, "Ain't that where we picked this fellow up?"

"Yup."

"Well, what the hell?"

"Maybe they're throwin' him back. Maybe he's too small a catch."

"Looks big enough to me."

They chuckled softly.

The driver maneuvered the ambulance skillfully as he sped toward the ocean. Drivers of cars, seeing the flashing red lights and hearing the siren, pulled to the curbs at either side as the ambulance whizzed by. They approached a red light at an intersection. Two cars, having the green, began to enter the intersection from either side.

"Watch it," one attendant said.

"Got it," the driver said.

At sixty miles per hour, the ambulance burst through the gap between the two cars, missing each by only a foot.

The driver spun the wheel to the left, careening around a corner, bumping the curb slightly.

"That's one," said his partner.

The driver swung into a right turn, brushing the other curb.

"That's two."

"You ain't never gonna see me hit three."

They sped past darkened houses and apartment buildings, into a neighborhood of single-story oceanfront homes. The driver swung to the left smoothly, the tires whining. Then he slowed as they passed an empty guard shack and wheeled into the big, empty, oceanfront parking lot. He glanced into the mirror. "Here?"

"Right to the water," Elizabeth barked. "Close as you can get."

"I'll put the wheels right in the water for you, if you want."

"I want."

He skidded the ambulance into a 180-degree turn and headed for a break in the fence where the boardwalk went through. They slipped through the fence with inches to spare, bumped across a wide strip of grass, and, with the two left wheels on the boardwalk, dipped down toward the surf. The ambulance slid sideways to a stop with the waves lapping over the wheels.

"Now what?" the driver asked.

"Just help us get him out of here," Elizabeth said.

The attendants went around to the back and opened the doors. They pulled the transporter out and lowered it into the edge of the water.

Elizabeth jumped down, followed by Doug.

"Now you guys can just back off. We'll handle it from here."

The attendants backed away from the water, looking down at their soggy shoes, and stood in the sand several yards away.

Elizabeth and Doug pulled the transporter until the water reached their thighs. Then they unbuckled the man and slid him off into the water, face down.

Doug helped Elizabeth mechanically, as if in a trance. Dimly he knew what she was doing, dimly he knew why, but his mind refused to accept it fully. He watched her put her hands under the man's shoulders.

She pulled him away. "I'll take it from here, Doug."

She dragged the man further out, her chiffon gown darkening in the water.

The two attendants gaped at the scene.

"She's drowning the guy."

"Sure looks that way."

"Shouldn't we do somethin'?"

"Nope. Must be Navy business. And keep your mouth shut about it too, just like the resident said back at the hospital."

"I ain't tellin' nobody. I don't even believe what I see."

Elizabeth was waist-deep in the water now, and waves splashed over her face. Her hair streamed dark and wet over her shoulders. She continued pulling the man forward under the water, now circling with him. She struggled, slow step by slow step, gagging occasionally as the waves hit her, but never ceasing to drag the man forward under the water, much as one might propel a sick shark to force water through its gills.

For several minutes she moved in a circular path, looking down at the man between waves. Doug watched dumbly from nearer the shore. The attendants on the beach stood rock still and staring.

For a time her legs ached, then they became numb. She sucked for breath in the brief spaces between waves, holding her breath when they hit her. Her eyes were fogged with exhaustion and salt spray. The man was heavy. Her hands cramped under his arms. She felt him slipping gradually from her.

She closed her eyes and tried to hold the weight. She kept plodding in a circle.

She was so weary that at first she didn't notice what was happening. It only slowly dawned on her that the man was no longer slipping through her hands. She was able to hold him firmly.

He was lighter.

She stared down at him, blinking the spray out of her eyes. He was much lighter now. His body was moving, the chest expanding and contracting with regularity.

More and more it became clear to her: he was breathing, under the water.

His weight became nothing. Cautiously, slowly, she slid her hands from him. He floated beside her, just under the surface, his body edging forward with slight eely undulations. He moved around her. She turned to follow him with her eyes.

He moved with painful slowness, the undulations of his body barely perceptible. It took him two full minutes to make one complete revolution around her.

Then for some moments he lay still in the water before her. Only then did she become conscious of the sounds of the waves and a few hovering gulls.

She dared not touch him; she could see that he was breathing, and beyond restoring that ability to him, she didn't know what she should do.

At last he rolled languorously over and faced her through the few inches of water above him. His eyes were open, and she saw them for the first time. His strange green metallic eyes were unblinking. The ebb and flow of the waves over him distorted Elizabeth's view of his face.

They stared at each other in this way for a time, Elizabeth oblivious to the waves washing over her. His face showed no emotion, only a blank expression. She could see that he was breathing steadily, and with strength. Gradually she began to smile at him. She felt herself smile as if it were an alien maneuver.

He did not smile. Nor did he blink or move his face at all. He just stared at her.

But then he moved a hand. He raised it slowly until it broke the surface. It was no longer black. He extended it up to her. Carefully she took it in her own. She did not try to pull him up, nor did he exert any force on her. He lay just under the water looking at her while she held his hand and smiled.

His hand was warm. Unconsciously she moved her thumb down to cover his pulse. It beat firmly. She felt herself laughing with joy.

She didn't even notice that between his fingers were small tissues of skin that webbed the fingers together.

She let him lie in the water for a long time. Then she gave his hand a gentle tug upward. He resisted, and she understood. He needed more time.

The first light of dawn was appearing over the hills when she pulled gently on him again. This time he allowed her to pull his arm up. He dropped his feet to the bottom and his head emerged from the water. The tide was low. Water drained off his well-muscled shoulders and chest.

She led him slowly out of the water and up onto the beach. His walk was unsteady, and he leaned on her for support.

She and Doug—who by then had recovered his wits—helped him into the ambulance, and he lay down on the transporter.

"Where to, ma'am?" the driver asked, his voice shaky.

"Undersea Center. You know where that is?"

"Yes, ma'am." He started the ambulance and churned back up the beach and through the parking lot onto the road.

"Listen, fellows," Doug crouched over their seat-back, "what happened here is not public business. It's Navy. You know the slogan, what you hear here, what you see here . . ."

"Stays here. Yes sir. We know it. We're secure."

"You better be. She's a general, you know."

"In the Navy?"

"Well, I'm not authorized to give you her real rank."

"Yes sir. We'll be at the center in a minute. Should I hit the siren?"

"No. And no lights. Just nice and easy."

"You got it."

## chapter 2

The Naval Undersea Center was a low, sprawling white complex of buildings at the side of a narrow, manmade ship channel. Two gray research vessels, bristling with electronic gear and winches and davits, were moored at the dock. Surrounding the buildings and their neatly tended yard was a twelve-foot, heavy-gauge chain-link fence. Two guards manned the entrance gate.

Inside the complex, in the various laboratories and water tanks, Elizabeth spent several days in near-total secrecy with her silent, newfound partner. She watched him swim and walk and exercise, monitoring his every movement and life system with instruments, scopes, and computers. She monitored him both awake and asleep, sleeping little herself, and never leaving the Center.

Few of the ranking officers knew what she was doing, even fewer knew any details of her work. Only two assistants aided her, but no one other than she knew everything she was working on. The arrangement was—and the Center brass trusted her implicitly, given her dedication and results over recent years—that when she was ready to report, she would report. And even then she would report only to those few she decided should hear the results of her testing of this strange man.

When she wasn't watching the man perform, or keeping her eye on the banks of monitors, she immersed herself in books. She kept notes in a shorthand only she could decipher.

That she was tired, near exhaustion, never occurred to her. For she was deeply, profoundly excited. She didn't know what her discoveries would mean to anybody, but she knew they would be important.

She wasn't quite sure herself why she insisted on such secrecy. It just seemed proper to keep all this under wraps at least until she knew what they were dealing with. And fortunately she didn't have to defend her demand for secrecy, because the Navy was most comfortable with secrecy, regardless of what it concerned. She thought of the Navy's attitude as being one craving not so much secrecy as privacy, like a club of experts who preferred to go about their work without kibitzers or meddlers or questioners.

She knew that some people thought she didn't like the Navy, or that it frustrated her. That wasn't true at all. It was just that the Navy wasn't her first love—research was. And where else but in the Navy could she have the opportunity to do the things she did? With the water-man, for example?

After her many days with him and the monitoring machines, she knew more about this "thing" or "being" or "man" than he probably knew about himself. She didn't know what to call him. "Thing" and "being" were far too cold. "Person" didn't quite fit either, because, although many of his systems were entirely human, some—most clearly the respiratory system—were not at all.

"Man" would be partially accurate. At least he looked like a man. He was six-feet one-inch tall, and weighed 182½ pounds. His muscles were long and firm, like—naturally enough—a swimmer's.

Except for the misleading suggestions of the word, Elizabeth would have described him as "handsome." Such a description was not scientific, however, so she kept that to herself. But he was: a strong face with fine, regular features and a square jaw; a body she would have described, unscientifically, as "perfect."

But there were other aspects of his looks that quickly set him apart from an ordinary human male. He had a nice head of black hair, but no hair at all on the rest of his body. His skin was smooth as a baby's, but much tougher.

Two physical qualities in particular made him obviously different. First and most noticeable were his eyes. They were, in a way, captivating, magnetic, haunting, intimidating. They were also, except for the small white spots in their centers, entirely green, with no apparent white sclera at all. If the white spots were pupils, Elizabeth's ophthalmoscope detected no contractions or dilations to accommodate changes in light—not when he was out of the water, in any case. The tear ducts were incompletely developed, by human standards. He didn't blink often and the eyes tended to dry out quickly when he wasn't submerged in the pool.

His eyes, like his muscles and his respiratory system, functioned best under water.

And the other external physical feature that distinguished him was even more patently aquatic: the webbing on his hands and feet.

The webbing between his fingers and toes was not

as extensive as a duck's. The tissue extended only halfway to his first knuckles, and was not immediately noticeable unless he spread his fingers wide. Under ordinary circumstances on land, a person not looking for the webbing would probably not notice it.

On land, where his gill-like respiratory system could tolerate his breathing for a few hours at a time, he moved about like a man, with strength and agility about normal for a man of his build and condition. But under water he was something else.

He didn't really swim as humans swim. He glided like an eel, undulating, with his arms tight to his sides and his legs together. And he moved at clearly inhuman speed. In the water, he displayed an agility and flexibility that suggested a body containing not firm bones but softer cartilage. That was an illusion, Elizabeth knew, for his body contained bones just like any human's. His style of swimming or gliding was not something he could have learned, but must have been innate. Like his strength. As normal as his strength was on land, under water he had enormous power. He could lift and pull tremendous weights.

Of all the things that puzzled Elizabeth, the difference between his physical abilities on land and in the water was not the most puzzling. The matter that intrigued her above all else was something to which she had no clue at all: where had he come from?

She had no clue because he never spoke. Whether or not he had some method for underwater communication she couldn't say; her instruments detected no vocal sounds. Still, he seemed to have quite human vocal equipment. Obviously he heard her speak, and he seemed to be able to follow her instructions. She didn't know if he could speak or not, or if he could, why he didn't.

But in so many ways he seemed like a human man that Elizabeth had to control her frustrations. Occasionally she found herself losing patience with him, perceiving him as just a man too stubborn to answer her. But for all that, he was cooperative, and terribly interesting.

For lack of any better terms, she applied those normal masculine ones—"he" and "him" and so forth —in referring to this tantalizing new creature, and came to think of him as more a human man than anything else, a man with highly individual characteristics, to be sure, a man so different that the Navy stamped him in his entirety as "classified."

She named him Mark Harris. She had determined to give him an unmistakably human name, one with no subtle aquatic implications; and a name which had personal associations for her. Mark was what she had always thought she would name a son, if she had one. She had lost interest in having a son when she had lost interest in getting married—which was when she realized her total involvement in her work, and recognized the fact that she could probably never devote herself entirely to one man.

Harris was the last man she had considered marrying, when she was in college. He was a Finnish lad from Connecticut, Harjis Pekkanen, whom everybody called "Harris." He was handsome and appealing and exciting in many ways, but he was weak and self-destructive. He wanted to be a writer, which was fine with her, but he would always start things he could not complete, or he would quit when success was near.

She had too positive an attitude to put up with that, too many things she wanted to accomplish, and believed she could accomplish to be dragged down by his negative attitude.

She had become more and more absorbed by medical and scientific research. And while she still enjoyed the company of men, they were, like the Navy, not her primary interest.

Mark Harris was the exception. To the extent that he was a "man," a man was now what dominated her interest.

She was under increasing pressure to reveal what she had discovered about Mark Harris. Those few Navy brass who had an inkling of what she was researching were anxious to learn about her discoveries. Curiosity was part of that; ego was a larger part. Ranking officers didn't like to think that something important was going on in their labs without their advice and control.

Elizabeth felt she could have gone on with her private research for month. Her knowledge was still advancing in small increments. But a major, crucial set of facts still eluded her and her computers and machinery and monitors: Who was Mark Harris really? Where did he come from? How did such a man-creature evolve?

Finally she sent word to Admiral Dewey Pierce—of whose domain the Undersea Center was part—in Washington, telling him that she was ready to give a presentation of her work to date.

In the conference room, Admiral Pierce, a white-haired, white-bearded, gimlet-eyed man of fifty, sat in a high-back leather swivel chair, an aide standing behind him, as Elizabeth narrated color slides.

Still photographs showed Mark in the water, and walking around the pool.

". . . After the second week he was able to leave the pool for short periods of time," she said, "and gradually those periods could be extended by several minutes. His general physical recovery and ability to perform under water were remarkable. It took somewhat longer for him to regain his equilibrium on land, and he was often reluctant to come out of the pool. For the most part, I deferred to his own inclinations to remain under water, both to gain his trust and because I supposed he knew best what he needed for being nursed back to health."

Then there were shots of Mark bare-chested in Navy work pants, being hooked onto testing machines—EKG, EEG, breathing apparatuses, exercise equipment.

". . . Then we began physiological studies. In these shots he is hard at work. But you will notice he doesn't show ordinary signs of exertion. He doesn't sweat, for example. Still, he did get tired, as you might expect.

The admiral took in the presentation without emotion. He stared intensely at the slides without commenting or even nodding. His aide, Lt. Ainsley, kept his eyes on the admiral, looking for reactions. Ainsley was fidgety, fearful that the admiral, because of his silence, might be growing impatient. He glanced at Elizabeth, who stood in her white lab coat with her arms folded.

Ainsley wished she would hurry up with the presentation, so that the admiral wouldn't suddenly turn grumpy and somehow blame him for the snail's pace of her report.

But the admiral, at this stage, showed nothing, and Elizabeth continued in her cool, professional, thorough manner.

". . . The evidence shows a humanoid being only marginally equipped for life on land . . ."

The trouble, Ainsley guessed, was that none of this really made sense, it couldn't really be true. He feared that the admiral would suddenly erupt in irritation at all this science fiction.

Slides now focused on Mark's various physical features.

". . . Testing indicates that his eyes are light-sensitive, but without expected adaptive changes while on land. We are preparing dichroic glasses for him. He sees best at greater depths, apparently. On land he tires comparatively easily, though, as I said, he does not sweat, his skin does not flush. But internal signs show rapid loss of energy while engaged in work on land. In addition, we find that within twelve hours out of the water, actual physical deterioration begins."

A slide showed a close-up of Mark's hands.

". . . Here we have the first stage of dehydration, the first signs of which are the prominent discoloration of the extremities . . ."

A series of slides showed the hands evolving from beige to tan to brown to chocolate and then to black.

". . . The latter stages of this change occur quite rapidly. We are unable to detect any signs of pain connected directly with this discoloration, although he does seem to suffer with attendant physical changes through this time . . ."

Slides showed him being assisted back into the pool.

". . . Within sixteen to twenty hours, if not returned

to a water environment, our projections are that the subject will suffer extensive skin cracking, pulmonary insufficiency, cardiac arrest, and death. We didn't actually keep him out of water that long, of course. But our monitoring of the early stages made these deductions quite reasonable. Even though the early stages of deterioration themselves must have been accompanied with some discomfort, the subject was remarkably cooperative, as if he wanted us to understand what could happen to him, his limitations, on land. However . . ."

"Doctor." Lt. Ainsley had been pacing quietly behind the admiral, and now was unable to restrain himself. "Perhaps we can finish off the technical side of the presentation. The admiral . . ."

"The admiral's doing just fine, Ainsley," Admiral Pierce said, swiveling around to him and smiling. He turned back toward the screen. "Go on, Doctor. And take your time. All this is fascinating, even if it is hard to absorb and accept."

"But sir," Ainsley stammered, "I—I was only thinking that . . ."

"If you can't sit still through this, Ainsley, you are welcome to take a walk."

"I'm fine, sir."

"Proceed, Doctor."

Elizabeth took a deep breath. "However, in the water a different picture emerges."

Shots showed Mark frolicking in the round pool, undulating gracefully, turning cartwheels in the water, diving straight down, rising straight up to break the surface, popping out to his waist, then arching over smoothly to dive again.

". . . He appears to be perfectly adapted to aquatic

life, displaying great strength and agility. He is as at home in the water as a fish, though with much greater strength, and, of course, with his brain and arms and legs, much greater flexibility and ability to perform all manner of underwater tasks. Better than any other truly aquatic mammal we know of—if we classify him as an aquatic mammal, which I am not yet prepared to do."

She gave the admiral a long look. "Because he's too much like a human man for me at this time to commit him to any other category, if you understand me."

The admiral nodded.

"Still, his capabilities underwater far surpass anything a human can do."

A slide showed Mark just emerged from the water, his smooth, hairless torso glistening with drops, his metallic green eyes with their typical piercing stare. A close-up showed his muscular chest.

". . . The chest cavity has gill-like membranes in place of normal lung tissue—"

"May I interrupt, Doctor?"

"Certainly, Admiral."

"Are you saying simply that he has gills rather than lungs?"

She stared at the screen thoughtfully. "Well, I wouldn't want to be quoted that way, Admiral. Without taking a biopsy or having the opportunity for, um—"

"An autopsy?"

"Yes. That is not to imply, of course, that I wish we *could* have an autopsy. I mean . . ."

"Of course, I understand. Nobody is wishing him dead, I assure you."

"What I mean to say is, without sampling tissues

and so forth, I would rather just say he has gill-like membranes through which he seems to absorb oxygen from the water."

"Simply put, Doctor, he breathes like a fish. Isn't that right?"

"Yes, sir."

"You needn't be coy about your findings, not with me."

"I know, sir, but it's just that I keep imagining some of this stuff as it would appear in newspaper headlines."

"Don't worry. It's all safe here."

"Yes sir."

"Continue."

She nodded and stepped to the screen and traced her finger around the image of Mark's chest. "His skin appears humanoid, but with certain dolphin characteristics."

Lt. Ainsley was ever more nervous over the science-fiction aspects of this presentation, and cast a sharp, incredulous look at her. The admiral's expression did not change.

". . . Except for his scalp, his body is completely hairless."

"No keratin layer in his skin?"

"None."

"Looks to me like he's wearing a wig," Ainsley muttered.

Elizabeth blinked slowly, controlling her desire to tell the young lieutenant to butt out. She turned to face him, and spoke evenly. "I can see just what you mean, Lieutenant. His hair lies very neatly on his head, and with the absence of hair elsewhere, one might wonder why he has it on his head. I wonder too. But he does. The sample we examined showed it to be entirely humanoid. Real hair. Like yours and mine. There are a lot of things for which I have no explanation. If you'll be patient with me, all I am trying to do at this point is show you what we've found so far. I hope we'll have answers to everything in time."

"Yes, ma'am. Sorry I interrupted." He hung his head.

"Don't be. I want to hear your questions, and answer them if I can."

"Proceed, Doctor."

"Right. Now, you've noticed that the hands and feet are webbed, which of course facilitates his movement underwater. We think the eyes may be catlike in deeper water. We suspect he may be able to see at ocean depths in almost total darkness. As with his other abilities, his vision is much more restricted on land. Except for bright sunlight, which may bother him a little, he seems able to see well enough without glasses."

She clicked in another slide, which showed Mark about a foot beneath the surface of the pool, lying face up, eyes closed, body still.

"What's happening there, Doctor?"

"He may be sleeping. At this moment we didn't have the monitors hooked up, but our data at other times indicates that he does sleep in that position, under water.

"I see. You've been able to keep him quite comfortably in the lab?"

"Yes sir. At the moment he's undergoing out-of-water fitness tests. We're continuing with all the tests, duplicating them, to get as good a fix on him as we can, before, unh, we have to end our tests. He's quite docile and cooperative—and I think he's becoming as curious about us as we are about him."

"Oh? How so?"

"Well, he hasn't spoken as yet, though he's obviously teachable and has vocal equipment. But he likes to examine our facilities, and he looks over the equipment quite carefully, as if he is very curious about it. And he listens carefully too, to me especially. He responds quickly, just so long as I explain everything beforehand. So, except for the fact that he doesn't actually ask questions, he clearly seems to be curious."

"You say he has vocal equipment."

"Yes sir, apparently fully developed."

"Do you have any theory on why he doesn't talk?"

"Not really. Except for obvious guesses. For example, he may never have spoken human language before. He may be shy until he knows it better."

"To say he's shy is to impute to him a quite human characteristic."

"I know. I'm sorry. I do that a lot. It is easy to think of him that way. But the fact is, he seems to understand so much of what I say that it's difficult to suppose that the language is entirely alien to him. Or perhaps he just chooses not to speak for some other reason, maybe self-protective, so as not to reveal himself too quickly. It's all pretty much guesswork just now, on that point. Maybe one day he'll surprise us all."

"What about his emotions?"

"Well, psychologically he appears cool and calm at all times. If he has emotions, he conceals them. At least from me, from what I can detect. He neither smiles nor frowns, for example. He shows no kind of impatience, even when our computers indicate that he may be straining or tired. But I'm reluctant to say he doesn't *have* emotions, since in fact we know so little about how his mind works."

"I agree with you."

"I'm glad you do, Admiral. I'm afraid others might want too quickly to categorize him in human terms."

"Speaking of human terms," the admiral swiveled back and forth, "is there any danger of you getting involved with him?"

"Sir?" Her face froze.

"Very handsome fellow, whatever he is."

"Sir," her voice turned cold, "I can safely say that there is no more danger of my 'getting involved with him,' as you say, than there would be if you were the attending scientist, and the subject were a woman."

"Oh, I don't know about that, if the subject were a woman just as nice-looking."

"Sir," she fixed her icy gaze on him, "I must beg your—"

"I'm teasing you, Dr. Merrill." His eyes twinkled. "No offense. Don't be so sensitive. Please continue with your presentation."

A bit unnerved, she turned back to the slides. The picture showed Mark Harris eating from a plate, rather clumsily holding his knife and fork over a serving of greens.

"His diet is kelp and plankton. I didn't have to guess too much at that. He had trouble with meat and potatoes, so I went right to kelp. He eats often, not much at a time. He drinks sea water, although he seems able to tolerate non-saline water, and milk. Coffee is out. It made him nauseous. At first we thought it might be because it was hot. But iced coffee had the same effect. So did tea. Coke too."

"They all have caffeine."

"Exactly. That's what we figure is the reason. Or one of them."

"If only he could, or would, talk."

"That would certainly save a lot of time. As for his origins, he's given us very little to go on. Nonverbal associative tests indicate possible amnesia."

"Amnesia?"

"Yes. And that makes everything tougher for us. Because we can never be sure whether something is really new to him, or he just forgot he knew it. We have no way of knowing whether he's ever been on land before, since apparently he has no need to leave the water."

"Then you're doing even better than I thought, figuring out as much as you have about him. Perhaps that even accounts for his not speaking, the amnesia."

"Perhaps."

The next slide showed a computer terminal.

"So we took every scrap of information we had and fed it to the WRW 12,000 at the Defense Department, and the computer sent back an answer. Sort of an answer."

A computer readout flashed onto the screen. ". . . LAST . . . CITIZEN . . . OF . . . ATLANTIS . . . ?"

She left the slide on and watched the admiral's expression. He narrowed his eyes and furrowed his brow as he gazed intently at the message.

"Atlantis," he said softly.

"We're not sure what that means, and frankly," her voice was calm, matter-of-fact, "we don't know if there are any more like him or not. But we know we have the absolute obligation to protect him while we're finding out everything we can about him."

"Atlantis," the admiral repeated, shaking his head slowly. "That would put him in the eastern Atlantic."

"Well . . ."

"And he was found in the eastern Pacific."

"Well," she gave a faint smile, "we're not sure about any of that, the Atlantis part. That's mythology, after all, even if it was Plato who first brought it up. And even if Plato was right, the island of Atlantis would have sunk into the Atlantic centuries ago, and people have been looking around the bottom all over from Gibraltar west for decades, without finding anything. Or without finding anything convincing. I don't know where the computer would have dug up such a story from its memory bank."

"Computers don't scorn mythology, if certain facts fit certain supposedly mythological circumstances."

"That's true, Admiral, but . . ."

"And you have no better theory to apply."

"Not yet, but . . ."

"So," he shrugged and smiled, "maybe he went through the Panama Canal."

She stared at him, watching him smile.

"In any event, Doctor, we have your computer's message, valid or not. We don't have to worry about it right now. We just put it in our own memory banks for storage."

She sighed finally and smiled back. "Good. For a moment I was just afraid you might think that I, that I . . ."

"That you believed it yourself? Relax. I admire you for having an open mind. You needn't pretend to have a closed one just to convince me you have a grip on reality."

"Thank you, Admiral."

"Now then. We've had a nice excursion into data and theory. I think this is all very exciting. Don't you, Ainsley?"

Ainsley, who had been listening to this latest dialogue with openmouthed amazement, suddenly straightened. "Oh, yes sir, definitely."

"So let's turn for a minute to something quite specific and practical. Doctor, I've got several pieces of underwater hardware put together by the best scientific geniuses in this country." His look turned sober. "This hardware is capable of lifting two thousand tons from a depth of twenty thousand feet. It can track a target in the ocean six miles down. It can take divers to a depth of three thousand, five hundred feet and bring them safely up again. Can your man do as well?"

Elizabeth stared at the wall. "I'm not sure."

"But," he smiled briefly, "I suspect you think it possible."

"Well, I . . . of course I'd like to know what he can really do. We haven't had the money to find out."

"You have it now."

She spun toward him, startled.

"Don't look so surprised. You're not as shocked as all that, Dr. Merrill. After all, you knew you were putting on a strong demonstration of your progress here this afternoon. You knew you would impress the man with the power to fund your program further."

She blushed. "I was only hoping," she said softly, "that you'd think I was doing a good job."

"How delightfully modest." He chuckled lightly. "Except that your statement is a bit disingenuous. Like all scientists, you want more money for your projects. Nothing wrong with that. Well, as I said, you have it. I like what you're doing. It's more important even than you may think. Now then, you say he's in the testing lab?"

"Yes sir."

"What say we all go have a look at your pet, Doctor."

"Of course." She ran her hand through her hair and took a deep breath. "Let's just ease in on him, though, so we don't disturb or frighten him."

"We'll just watch quietly, like good little boys."

"Fine," she said firmly.

The young lab assistant finished his cup of coffee, stood up, stretched, and checked the stopwatch that dangled around his neck. He picked up his clipboard, went out of the galley and down the hall toward the testing lab.

He pushed open the door, turned immediately to his right, and headed toward the bank of monitors at one end of the room, not looking at the treadmill rumbling at the other end.

"Okay, Mark, you can stop now. Time's . . ." He glanced back at the treadmill now and stopped, stunned.

The treadmill was running, but Mark was not running on it. He was gone. The door behind it leading to the dressing room was ajar.

The technician trotted toward it. "Mark? Mark?"

Mark's locker was open and his clothes were gone. All that was left on the bench in front of his locker was the pair of running shorts he had worn to work on the treadmill.

The technician sank back against the wall and stared at the open locker. "Oh my dear Lord," he moaned. "It had to be me."

Then he sprang into action, running out of the lab and down the hall. The first person he had to find was Dr. Merrill, before he would even begin the search for Mark Harris. And while he ran through the corridor, scenes of his entire naval career flashed before his eyes, all two years, four months, seven days, and six hours.

For a moment Mark Harris stood outside the main Center building, just beyond the front steps. He was wearing an ordinary Navy work outfit, and dark glasses. He looked around the grounds, blinking occasionally behind the glasses when he faced the sun.

A group of young Navy men came around the corner and headed toward the gate, jabbering and laughing among themselves. Mark fell in behind them. He walked with a rolling gait, turning his head from side to side to take in his new world.

The group, with Mark at the rear, waved at the guards as they passed through the gate. Mark copied their moves exactly.

They walked down the street. A blue Navy truck rumbled toward them, and they all stepped out of its way onto the sidewalk.

Except for Mark. With a screeching of brakes, the truck came to a halt a few feet in front of him. The driver leaned out.

"Where the hell you walkin', monkey? This ain't no pedestrian mall! Move it!"

Mark stared back at him.

"Come on, move it!"

The driver waved his arm toward the sidewalk, and then Mark responded quickly, hopping onto the walk. The driver shook his head, shoved the truck into gear, and moved on. Mark stared after him.

He looked around for the other Navy personnel he had been following, but they were gone.

Elizabeth walked beside Admiral Pierce and in front of Lt. Ainsley as they headed toward the lab where she had left Mark to work out.

"I just hope I told you everything," she said. "There was so much to condense into so short a time."

"Please, you did magnificently. Nobody expects to learn in an hour everything that's taken you weeks. You told me enough."

"It just seemed so strange, in a way. I'd got quite used to him and his idiosyncrasies from my daily contact. But then it seemed so strange to be actually telling it all to somebody . . ."

"Dr. Merrill! Dr. Merrill!" The lab assistant came flying breathlessly down the corridor toward them. He skidded to a stop on his heels. "Unh," he took her arm and looked wildly at her. "I gotta talk to you, alone!"

"Go ahead, it's okay. What is it? Calm down." But she herself was already trembling, knowing instantly that it had to be some emergency.

"Mark's gone!"

She stepped back.

"Who's Mark?" the admiral asked.

"I forgot to tell you we had given him a name . . ."

Mark stayed on the sidewalks now, virtually clinging to them as he saw people do. He barely dared to cross the streets, and did so only in company with others. He saw more and more people as he approached the town.

His eyes took in everything; everything was new to him. Cars and trucks, people of all shapes and sizes dressed in every imaginable color; grass and trees and concrete; signs and lights and posters; bicycles and motorcycles and parking meters; telephone poles and lines; stores with goods displayed behind glass.

People moved around him every which way, in confusing patterns, not in familiar schools. So occupied was Mark with observing everything that occasionally he bumped into somebody. He moved quickly away from such confrontations, learning to grunt in response like those he bumped into.

He tried to fall into the patterns of walking, following people who were in any way bunched or even in twos, if they seemed to be headed in some rather constant direction.

He followed a cluster of three into the revolving door of a bank. He found himself propelled not into the bank, but all the way around in the door until he was back outside. He watched two others enter the bank, then stepped into the door and managed to get inside. He stood behind the two men as one by one they transacted business with a teller.

Then Mark stood before the caged window, staring at the teller.

"May I help you?" the young woman asked.

Mark just stared.

"Sir?" Slowly she eased off her chair and walked away. She tapped a guard on the shoulder. "That Navy guy over there," she whispered, gesturing discreetly behind her, "is acting suspiciously."

"Who?"

When she turned around, Mark was gone.

He exited through the revolving door, looked up and

down the street, and turned to his right to walk toward a Jack-in-the-Box drive-in restaurant. He kept his eyes on the metal clown which stood next to the building.

He walked up the driveway and looked at the clown face smiling down at him. The gravelly voice said, "May I take your order, please?"

He stared at the face.

"May I take your order, please?"

A car pulled up behind Mark. The horn tooted, startling him. He spun around toward it. A second car pulled up behind the first.

"May I take your order, please?"

Three horns now tooted. Mark backed away, turned, and walked off down the street.

He moved more quickly now, more nervously. Still he looked from side to side to take in the sights, but he eyed things more warily. Ahead of him a man stepped out of a glass phone booth.

As Mark neared the booth, he heard the phone ringing.

He stepped into the booth, the door sliding shut behind him. He stared at the jangling phone. Slowly he reached out and touched the receiver. The phone rang again, and he snatched his hand back from the vibration. When that ring stopped, he picked up the receiver and looked at it.

"One moment, please," came the operator's voice, "for overtime charges."

Hearing the voice, he put the receiver against his ear. But there was silence. He held it in front of him, and the voice returned.

"That'll be one dollar and forty-five cents additional, please."

Mark put the phone to his ear again, and again heard nothing. The voice returned when he held the receiver in front of him.

"Hello? Are you the party that placed the call to Seattle, Washington?"

Quickly he put the receiver to his ear. This time the voice continued.

"Hello? Hello? Is this the party who . . ."

A rap on the glass caused him to drop the receiver.

He turned to see a small boy standing outside the booth, gazing at him. The boy motioned for him to come out. The sign on the side of the door facing Mark said *Pull.* Mark pushed at the door. He pushed harder. He turned and pushed at the walls of the booth. His eyes began flicking right and left. His hands clenched.

The boy rapped again. Mark smacked the door with his palms.

Then the boy reached out and gently pushed the door open. Mark stood staring down at the boy, breathing heavily. The boy smiled. Mark quickly slid past him out of the booth.

The slightest tinge of darkness appeared at the ends of his fingers. He scanned the horizon. He saw the tops of the communications antennae that rose over the Undersea Center to the west.

He walked off quickly in that direction, his rolling gait a bit unsteady.

"No, Admiral, I'm sorry, but I must insist that there be no general alarm!"

"But Doctor, we've got to find him as quickly as possible, as you yourself said."

"Yes. But not that way. We just can't have armed guards who know nothing about him chasing him down."

"But how . . ."

"We have to do it ourselves." She started toward the main entrance door, moving at a near trot.

The admiral and lieutenant trotted behind her. The lieutenant put a hand on the admiral's arm. "Sir," he whispered, "should I put the alarm out anyway?"

"No." The admiral caught up with Elizabeth. "Dr. Merrill, hold it a second."

They stopped together near the door. Elizabeth stood uneasily, her eyes flitting back and forth from the admiral to the door. She began to edge closer to the door.

"Doctor, I'm willing to defer to you on matters relating to this project. But really, we can't just race out there willy-nilly. We have no idea where he might have gone, which direction, nothing."

"Admiral, he's running out of time."

"I understand, but . . ."

"Which means that either he will come back here—which I admit is unlikely—or he'll head toward the ocean."

"But he could have gone straight out there to the dock and already have gone into the ocean right there."

"No. Take a look out there." They all turned to look out the glass doors. "The guards are in their positions, just as if nothing happened. Everything looks normal. He didn't go into the water there. He must have walked away, just like a normal Navy man. We'll find him. Please!"

"Let's go."

They pushed open the doors, then stopped short.

"Mark!"

He was coming up the steps toward them, his labored breathing apparent. He stopped and stared at them, then he put a darkened hand to his chest.

"Help him inside! We've got to get him into the pool!" She took one of Mark's arms, the admiral took the other. "Try not to make it obvious."

They quickly brought him inside, steered him through the corridors, and out the back door. At the edge of the round pool they released him. He quickly slid into the water and submerged, fully clothed.

"Close," Elizabeth said, panting.

"Lucky." The admiral nodded. "Or maybe it wasn't luck. He must trust you enormously, to come back like this."

"Let's hope so."

"That's terribly important, for him to trust you completely."

"You mean for the research."

"And the usefulness of it, the applications."

"How so?"

The admiral didn't answer. He squatted down beside the pool and watched Mark moving underwater. He had recovered quickly, and was gliding around gracefully. He stopped underwater to remove his clothes, leaving on only his tight swim trunks. Then he resumed his undulating swim.

They watched silently for a while. Then Mark's head broke the surface. He moved slowly over to the side near them, and looked up at Elizabeth. She nodded to him. He took another dive, and resurfaced beside them.

Elizabeth knelt down beside the admiral. "Mark,

this is Admiral Pierce." Mark slowly turned his head toward the admiral, who nodded to him. "He's come here from Washington, from our government headquarters, to meet you. He's a very understanding man, a very important man, and he's going to help you. He's going to help us get to know each other better."

Mark backpedaled a few feet and stared at the admiral. Then he looked at Elizabeth.

"It's all right, Mark. He's a friend. He is a very important friend. You can trust him."

Mark ducked under the water and dove for the bottom. They could barely make out his outline, shimmering fifteen feet down.

"What now?" the admiral asked.

"Give him time."

"All right."

They waited beside the pool as Mark lay submerged at the bottom. Then he began moving around the floor, swimming laps just above it. For twenty more minutes he stayed near the bottom. Then gradually he made his circles higher, moving toward the surface.

His head and torso emerged right in front of Admiral Pierce.

Elizabeth smiled. "Admiral, meet Mark Harris."

The admiral got down on his knees. Lt. Ainsley winced when he saw the knees of the admiral's bright, white ducks scrape on the concrete.

The admiral stuck out his hand toward Mark. "How are you, son?"

Mark looked at the hand, then at the admiral's face. He did not reach out to take the hand.

The admiral studied the deep, green eyes, and withdrew his hand. "I'm very glad to meet you, Mark. I'm pleased that you are working so well with Dr.

Merrill here." Their eyes remained locked. "I hope to see a lot more of you. I'm sorry you went away from the laboratory for a while. You caused us quite a scare. I'm sorry too that your wanderings," he smiled slightly, "caused you to run out of gas."

Mark shifted his gaze to Elizabeth. She smiled down at him.

"We're glad to see you're feeling better now, Mark. Why don't you pick up your clothes from the bottom and hand them to me. I'll get them dry. You can stay in the pool for as long as you want. Okay?"

Mark quickly dipped under the water and dove straight down like an arrow, snatched up his clothes, surfaced in an instant, and handed them to Elizabeth. Then he retreated to the bottom where he lay on his back, looking up at them, the refraction of light in the water causing his image to waver. But his unblinking eyes glimmered steadily like twin beacons.

The admiral stood up. Ainsley quickly stooped to brush off his knees.

"Well, Doctor, we've had not only an excellent presentation by you, but an adventure to boot, and a marvelous display in the water by your Mark Harris." He did not smile. "It's been quite a day. Now then. There's a lot to do. I want some very specific information in the coming days. I want to know his underwater speed, agility, strength, and stamina. Not in general terms, but in absolute limitations so far as you can determine them. You've got whatever funds you need. Start testing him right away."

"Yes sir."

"Ainsley."

"Yes sir?"

"Take those clothes of his and see to getting them

dry. We'll leave the good doctor to more important tasks."

"Aye-aye, sir." Ainsley took the clothes.

The admiral spun smartly on his heel and walked off toward the gate.

Ainsley looked at the clothes, which were dripping onto his shiny black shoes.

"There's a dryer in the east wing, Lieutenant."

"Thank you, ma'am." He looked up at her. "I hope you'll excuse me for butting in now and then, back at the presentation. But I'm supposed to keep things moving smartly for the admiral, because if things drag, he gets cranky, and—"

"Forget it, Lieutenant. Glad you came."

"Um, one other thing, Dr. Merrill." He looked shyly at the ground. "I'm supposed to stick around here, with you. The admiral wants me to help keep an eye on him." He cocked his head toward the pool.

"I understand." She pondered the glistening surface of the pool, and Mark's shivering image deep within it. "Tell me something, Lieutenant."

"Ma'am?"

"What is the admiral's primary interest?"

"Well, I don't know that I can speak for the admiral . . ."

"I mean, what did he tell you was his purpose for coming out here?"

"National defense."

Elizabeth nodded slowly and closed her eyes. When she looked back at the pool to see Mark's head poke out from the rippling water, her eyes had a touch of disappointment in them.

## chapter 3

"Phil, nobody knows better than I how strange it sounds. But it is not impossible. Human breathing is not so far removed from that of fish."

"Oh, come on, Elizabeth," Lieutenant Commander Roth looked at her over his glass of wine, "that's like comparing apples and oranges. You might as well say a man breathes like a bug—everything needs oxygen. But fish get their oxygen from the water. People can't do that. And the way you describe him, he's practically human."

"He is similar to a human male, Phil, except for certain aspects. Foremost among the ways he is different is that he doesn't have human-type lungs. Our pictures of his insides show that rather than two human tissue pouches called lungs, he has in his chest layers and layers of membrane that look a lot more like gills."

"You're going on looks alone?"

"Looks and behavior. After all, we can't just open him up and take those tissues out and examine them under a microscope. They *appear* to be similar to gills. And he appears to breathe under water."

"What do you mean, appears to?"

"Well, he can stay submerged for hours at a time—

apparently indefinitely. Wouldn't that suggest to you that he breathes under water?"

"Okay. So he's a fish, then. All he needs is some scales on his body, and some big lips. Then we could just dump him back in the water and forget about him."

"Oh Phil," she smiled, "you always have to have things so cut and dried. Things have to be totally one way or totally the other for you. No, he's not a fish. Yes, I think he breathes like a fish. But what I'm trying to tell you is that with certain alterations in lung structure, so could anybody. There's not that much difference."

"You need some more wine, my dear." Phil reached for the bottle of Bordeaux Supérieur. "Your project is getting the best of you." He refilled her glass, and the dark red wine sparkled in the light of the candle. "You get enough to eat?"

"I sure did." She leaned back and stretched. "Your veal piccata is still marvelous. You haven't lost your cooking touch. You must be entertaining a great deal."

"Piccata is like swimming. Once you've learned, you never forget. We've got mousse coming up, don't forget." He sipped his wine. "Tell me why it is so easy for a man to breathe like a fish, dear Doctor."

"You mean a man with respiratory structure more like gills than lungs."

"Okay. So tell me about it."

"I'll try. There are a lot of things we still don't understand completely. Don't get impatient if I start with basics, which you already know, to build my case."

"Am I ever impatient?"

"No, Phil," she chuckled, "never."

"So hurry up and tell me then." He chuckled back.

"All right. Humans breathe by taking oxygen and nitrogen into the lungs. Those gasses filter through the lung wall and are taken into the blood. Carbon dioxide is released by the blood back through the lung wall, and is breathed out. Fish do the same, except that they breathe in water instead of air, and the oxygen and nitrogen in the water pass through the gill membranes into the blood, and carbon dioxide passes back through the gill membranes and re-enters the water. Okay?"

"So what else is new? So far it's high school science."

"Right. Now, the reason that exchange of oxygen with the blood and air takes place in humans is that the pressure of oxygen in the *air* is greater than the pressure of oxygen in the blood, so oxygen tends to move from the air through the lung wall into the blood. At the same time, the pressure of carbon dioxide in the *blood* is greater than that in the air, so the carbon dioxide tends to leave the blood through the lung wall and enter the air."

"Elizabeth . . ."

"You agreed to let me start with the basics."

"Okay, okay. Anyway, I can look at you while you talk, which is always a pleasure."

"But listen too, okay?"

"Promise."

"Now, the molecules of oxygen and nitrogen dissolved in water have about the same pressure as in the free air, and they move in about the same rapid motion. So they can pass from water through the gill membranes of a fish the same way they pass through the lung membranes in humans. The difference basically is only that there are fewer molecules of oxygen per cubic foot of water than per cubic foot of air. So, to breathe water, more membrane must be in contact with the water to get enough oxygen."

"Did I ever tell you that your eyes are even more beautiful when you are deeply absorbed in your subject?"

"Hey!"

"I'm listening."

"Yeah, I can tell."

"No, really, Elizabeth. I follow you on the oxygen-transfer bit, the difference between water and air."

She leaned back and sighed. "I should give you a quiz afterward."

"Fine. That means you'll be here longer."

"To continue, with your permission . . ."

"Granted."

"Whereas a human has just two lungs, each with a singular surface, quite sufficient for extracting oxygen from the air, that total surface area is not enough for water. A fish, on the other hand, has layers and layers of gill membrane—a much greater amount of the membrane in relation to the size of the fish—for the water to wash over continually for oxygen extraction. To put it quite simply, a human drowns in water because although the lung apparently can extract enough oxygen from the first breathful of water, there cannot be maintained a sufficient circulation of water to renew the oxygen supply. There simply isn't enough lung surface to be in contact with the water. A fish out of water cannot breathe sufficient oxygen because it doesn't have expanding lungs to draw in the air, and because the gill tissues must be kept moist to function properly."

"Just to show you that I'm listening, Elizabeth, let me point out that you completely ignore certain facts, such as the differences in the lung and gill membranes themselves—not only their structure but their fabric—and the differences in muscular structure, and—"

"Yes, yes, yes, I'm aware of all that, my favorite lieutenant commander. I'm just trying to show you that the basic breathing functions in humans and fish are not as different as most people assume. In fact, it has actually been proven that, given the proper type of membrane and enough surface of it, a human can actually breathe under water."

"Proven? Come on . . ."

"Proven, Phil. The Navy's been playing with this concept for twenty-five years or so. And others have tried it out too. You don't have to believe what I say about Mark Harris. These are things you can look up yourself. For example, in the early sixties an inventor from New Jersey named Waldemar Ayres built a gill apparatus that actually worked. He made four fifteen-foot-long panels of plastic membrane that allowed gasses from the water to pass through them, but not the water itself. Sixty-four square feet of this membrane were in contact with the water. Using a scuba-type breathing hose attached to this artificial gill, he breathed oxygen extracted from the water for more than an hour."

"Where on earth did you hear a thing like that?"

"As I said, you can look it up. And if that doesn't tell you something, there's more. In 1964, General Electric built a small animal cage covered with a thin silicone rubber membrane. They put a hamster in the cage and submerged the whole thing under water for a long time, and the hamster breathed. That means that the oxygen was filtering through the membrane into the cage. And theoretically, with a big enough bubble of the right membrane, a man could be safely submerged in it the same way."

"That's not much like a gill."

"It's exactly the same principle, Phil, just that in these cases the gill was an external one, not one inside the chest. But the effect was exactly the same."

"You said I could look this stuff up. Where? In *Science Fiction Digest*?"

"Not at all. The GE experiments were covered by *Life* magazine, *Time, The New York Times, Scientific American,* and a bunch of other publications."

"And what about this other guy, what's his name?"

"Ayres. Well, in 1966 he got a patent on his device, which means he had to demonstrate that it worked. And his patent even covered the method used by GE."

"Hey, Elizabeth," his tone suddenly changed, "you really mean it, don't you?"

"Of course. I'm a scientist myself, you know, and I have the same questions you do."

"But why wasn't something done with all this? Why hasn't the whole underwater business been revolutionized? Why are we still diving with compressed-air tanks instead of using some of these artificial-gill-type things?"

"Aha. Now it's my turn to inject a bit of what you might call 'reality.' The question was—as it usually is—one of money and practicality. Theoretically, a man, using an artificial gill of this type properly designed to be strapped to his back, could swim around under water indefinitely, breathing like a fish, with no air tanks or surface hoses or anything. But nobody seemed to want to invest the money to develop such a usable backpack gill, because one major problem remained."

"Which was?"

"The artificial gills would work for humans only in relatively shallow water. The deeper you dive, the more nitrogen is absorbed into your system. The ordinary human diver using compressed-air tanks begins to suffer from nitrogen narcosis at around a hundred feet, and it gets worse the deeper you go. For some it starts much shallower."

"You and I have both been through that drunken euphoria enough times. 'Rapture of the depths,' such a beautiful, deceptive term."

"I'll say. Well, the problem is, the artificial gill doesn't change that. You still get too much nitrogen in deep dives. And the other problem is with the bends. On longer dives—beyond, say, thirty feet—you would still have to go through gradual decompression from the added depth pressures before you could surface. So in simple terms, the artificial gill might allow you to breathe like a fish, but you would still be subject to human limitations. And aside from allowing you to swim in shallow water without air tanks or hoses, an artificial gill wouldn't change the problems scuba divers have always had."

"But still, Elizabeth, most diving is done in less than twenty-five feet of water. You would think that somebody would want to develop a gill even if it's just for that."

"You would think. I guess it would cost a lot of money. When Ayres got his patent, he made a deal with some company to develop his artificial gill. The word is that the Navy was going to underwrite the project with the company, to provide lab facilities and so forth. But then the Navy backed out—maybe because they didn't feel that the possible military applications would justify the money—and the project just sort of disappeared."

"And now you have your project. And this Mark Harris, with his—as you call them—'gill-like tissues,' he can do all this underwater breathing without these problems. I wonder why."

"I wish I had the answers. In the first place, though, what he breathes with is not artificial. The components of the membrane may be crucial, for instance. And he doesn't get nitrogen narcosis or the bends. I don't know why. In that way he's more like a fish."

"All like a fish, as I see it."

"Nope. Because he can also breathe satisfactorily on land for quite a long while."

"At least he's totally different from humans as far as water is concerned."

"You make it sound like all humans are just alike in that regard."

"Well aren't they? Given proper conditioning and training, we all dive the same way, experience the same effects."

Elizabeth laughed lightly and tilted her head toward the ceiling. "Dear old Phil, I can't believe what I hear you say. You know full well that thin people tend to suffer nitrogen narcosis more quickly than heavier people, because fatty tissue can absorb more nitrogen safely."

"Well, okay, I know, but . . ."

"Perhaps you don't know—but you should—that there is some evidence that women may be naturally better adapted to diving and swimming than men."

"How so?"

"Because the greater amount of fatty tissue in women's chests and legs makes them naturally more buoyant than men. So while a man uses more energy just to stay horizontal under water, a woman can use her energy to move around, to swim, to work."

"Oh come on, Liz," Phil wrinkled up his nose and frowned, "a man has more powerful muscles and—"

"So?" She interrupted and leaned over the table and touched his nose with the tip of her finger. "You will admit that there are differences even in humans, under water?"

"Touché." He smiled and took her hand. "Anyway, now you've really got me interested in your project."

"I don't have to remind you," she withdrew her hand gently, "that this is a top-security matter."

"Thanks for reminding me that you don't have to remind me. I am a lieutenant commander in your same navy, after all. And who would I tell? I'll be gone taking the *Sea Quest* on a dive soon anyway."

"Really? Where to?"

"I don't know, for sure. I just know it's gonna be super-deep."

"When?"

"Maybe in a week or so. They've been keeping it under wraps. We're getting a full briefing from Defense on Monday."

"That's great. I hope your machine works."

"Oh, she'll work. You ready for your mousse? It's all chilled."

She stood up and stretched. "Let me pass on it this time, Phil. I'm still stuffed with veal. And I've got to be getting back. We'll be starting a new series of performance tests tomorrow. I've got some paperwork to get through."

"Okay. Sorry you're leaving, but glad you came. As you know."

"Thanks, Phil." She slipped on her light sweater, and he walked her to the door. "I'm glad I came too. This is the first time I've been out of that lab for weeks. It feels good."

"In a few days, when I get back from my dive, will you come over, and stay longer?"

"Sure. You'll have a lot to tell me about. And I'll eat the mousse. Bon voyage."

"Till then."

Mark and a dolphin, brown and friendly, cavorted in the long, rectangular dolphin pool, diving under and over each other, rolling on their backs, swimming together in circles.

"Hey, Mark," Elizabeth, in a diver's wet suit, stooped at the edge of the pool, "save your strength for the tests. You'll both be worn out before you can show your stuff."

Admiral Pierce and Lt. Ainsley walked up behind her and watched as Mark separated himself from the dolphin and glided over to Elizabeth.

She looked up and blushed slightly. "I was only teasing him, Admiral. Actually I'm not worried about Mark. He's got tremendous endurance. In the water, that is."

"Well, that's one of the things we're here to see. Does he understand how to run through these tests, what they're all about?"

"I don't know if he understands what they're all about, sir, but he knows how to do them. So, by the way," she smiled, "does the dolphin."

"Dolphins are too darn friendly for their own darn

good, sometimes." The admiral watched the dolphin leaping around the pool.

"How do you mean?"

"Oh, just that we've had some difficulty teaching them to be a little more, unh, aggressive, you might say, in certain situations. I'm speaking about defense work, of course. Personally I like the little buggers. But in certain situations where we want them to be a little more, unh, helpful against a hostile subject, they turn out to be altogether too palsy-walsy. I'm hoping your, er, man might have a more finely tuned sense of discrimination in his behavior."

"I don't know about his aggressiveness, Admiral. I've never seen him get hostile. He certainly is co-operative. He'll do anything I ask."

"Well, let's get on with it. Let's see what he can do when I'm around."

"Okay." She leaned over toward Mark, who had been studying the admiral's face. "Mark, we're going to do the speed and agility tests now, okay? Even more than before. It is important for the admiral to see for himself what you can do."

Mark slid under the water, swam over and nudged the dolphin, and together they moved to the shallow end of the pool. Elizabeth dropped in beside the dolphin and petted it as it nuzzled her leg.

Her lab assistant, crouched at the edge of the far end of the pool, held a small bell in one hand and a stopwatch in the other. Beside him was a small bucket of fish.

At the side of the pool opposite the admiral and Ainsley, a Navy man in work clothes adjusted his small movie camera atop its tripod and focused it on Mark and the dolphin, then turned it slowly to scan the length of the pool. He gave Elizabeth the thumbs-up sign.

"Okay, everybody ready?" She looked at the admiral, who nodded, and at her assistant, who held up the bell. "Ready, Mark?" Mark and the dolphin separated a few feet, lay still in the water, heads toward the far end.

Elizabeth held up her palm toward the assistant while she checked the alignment of Mark and the dolphin, then clenched her hand into a fist.

The assistant rang the bell. Instantly Mark and the dolphin surged forward, both lightning-fast. Mark's undulating movements more pronounced than the dolphin's.

In seconds they arrived at the end of the pool, turned together, zoomed back to the shallow end, turned again, and raced back to the assistant. They arrived virtually simultaneously at the far end. The assistant dipped his hand toward Mark, indicating that he had arrived a fraction of a second before the dolphin.

The admiral looked amazed. Lt. Ainsley's mouth hung open.

The assistant reached into the bucket and took out a tiny fish. He tossed it out over the pool. Mark propelled himself straight up from the water, grabbed it with his left hand, and flipped it toward the dolphin, who leaped up and caught it in its mouth and swallowed it.

Elizabeth beamed at the admiral.

"Amazing, Dr. Merrill. Truly amazing. You get it all on there, cameraman?"

The photographer across the pool nodded and waved.

"Let's do it again, Doctor."

Elizabeth lined up Mark with the dolphin, and the race was repeated, with the same result.

"Again."

Again they raced, finishing exactly together.

"I'm convinced of his speed, Doctor," the admiral said, coming around to her end of the pool and extending a hand to help her out. "You were absolutely right, no exaggeration. Exciting." He lifted his head to look out to the center of the pool, where Mark was floating on his back. "Excellent, Mr. Harris. Thank you." He gave Mark a snappy salute.

Mark swung his legs down under him and gazed at the admiral, then at Elizabeth.

"Perfect, Mark," she called out.

Mark flipped upside down, kicked his legs high out of the water, and dove for the bottom.

"Now, Dr. Merrill, we have some more difficult tasks for him. Even more profound in meaning. You'll have him ready for the CURV tests early tomorrow morning?"

"Yes sir. Mark will be ready whenever the CURV is."

"It's set to go. They're dropping the dummy torpedoes in the channel this afternoon."

At the mention of torpedoes, an apprehensive look flicked across Elizabeth's face. But she said nothing. She joined the admiral to walk back into the laboratory.

"Tell me, Doctor, I'm curious about your man's sensitivities. You've swum with him, I assume."

"Many times."

"How does he behave, in the water with you?"

"It's quite interesting, actually. When I have tanks,

he swims around all over the place, does whatever I signal him to do. When I go under without tanks, he seems reluctant to leave me alone—as if he knows I don't belong under the water that way, because I can't breathe without the tanks."

"Which indicates, of course, that he does have some emotions after all."

"Well, I think he knows that I can't breathe under water like he does. I suppose he can only guess at my capacities. But he knows I can't stay under too long, without an airpack. I guess you might say he shows some concern for my safety."

"That is encouraging. I had hoped he had something approaching human intelligence. Very valuable."

"This might surprise you, Admiral, but in fact that dolphin behaves the same way, when I'm under water."

"Is that so? Perhaps the dolphin picked that up from him."

She shook the water out of her hair and stepped through the door, which the admiral held open for her. "Perhaps."

"Does he ever physically try to assist you in any way in the water, lift you or support you or anything?"

"You mean with his arms?"

"Yes."

"Mark has never touched me, nor I him, except to shake hands. And except when I've examined him, of course."

"But of course his *having* arms gives him a tremendous advantage, in performing tasks."

"You mean advantage over a dolphin."

"Yes."

"Naturally."

"So I'm excited at the prospect of testing his strength and dexterity, with those arms."

"That'll be tomorrow."

"Yes. See you in the channel."

Elizabeth spent a restless night. She slept on a cot in her office at the lab. She too was anxious to discover and show off Mark's various talents and capabilities. She had a strong proprietary interest in him; he was her very own project, her star. The advancement of her career was intertwined with Mark's performance.

Yet, Mark was not "hers," not just some piece of scientific gear. So at the same time she was apprehensive about how his talents might be used. There was always the bottom line of what the Navy existed for. She felt herself wishing—almost—that he would show some vulnerability, some flaw or weakness under water that would make him unacceptable for certain tasks, and keep him out of the clutches of those who might misuse his skills.

Still, she knew that, as with so many aspects of scientific exploration, the job of the scientist is to advance knowledge even when the dissemination of that knowledge might lead to something destructive. And so she had no choice but to proceed in discovering and presenting the very best of everything Mark could do.

For all this restless nighttime musing, she didn't really feel morbid about it. The negative aspects were nothing more than faint vibrations in the air. The positive excitements and pride of discovery were thrilling and rewarding. And she looked forward to every day. Especially tomorrow, when for the first time

Mark would be tested adequately and realistically on his deep-water abilities.

The two red marker buoys bobbed in the water one hundred yards off the end of the channel, fifty yards apart. Nearby, a buoy tender sat bulkily in the water. Elizabeth and Admiral Pierce and several other Navy personnel stood on the low, broad deck and watched the two scuba divers slip into their tanks and test their breathing regulators. Mark, in a Navy wet suit without tanks, stood at the railing looking out over the Pacific, his arms folded across his chest.

An ensign trotted down the steps from the bridge and came over to Admiral Pierce. "Sir, bridge reporting CURV is in the area." He stuck his arm out toward the southwest, palm vertical, fingers straight, indicating a vector toward the invisible CURV—Cable Controlled Underwater Recovery Vehicle—which would be approaching the buoys deep under water. "CURV is ready to proceed with recovery on your signal, sir."

The admiral nodded. "Stand by for my signal."

They saluted each other, and the ensign stood aside at attention.

"Okay, Doctor, it's your show."

"Divers ready?"

The two divers gave thumbs-up. They picked up their underwater movie cameras and moved to the diving ladder. They stuck their regulators into their mouths and adjusted them.

"All right. Let's go. Dive!"

The first diver splashed in on his back and disappeared under the swells, followed quickly by the second. Two trails of air bubbles followed them away from the ship toward the buoys.

Elizabeth checked her stopwatch. She walked over to Mark. "Ready, Mark?"

He looked at her, then walked over to the diving ladder.

She checked her watch again. "All right, Admiral, the divers should be in position."

The admiral turned to the ensign. "Proceed with CURV recovery mission."

The ensign saluted and raced up to the bridge.

"Okay, Mark," Elizabeth said, "go."

Mark dove in headfirst, making virtually no splash, and disappeared.

Elizabeth lifted her binoculars and scanned the area under which Mark and the CURV could work. But there was nothing to be seen. They would just have to wait.

The divers, hovering four fathoms above the bottom, first saw the CURV approaching several feet below them. The silvery CURV looked like a giant insect as it moved along just over the ocean floor. Its lights burned a path ahead of it. Two large cameras looked like square eyes on a head filled with insect-like antennae. Its segmented metal arm resembled a huge lobster claw.

One diver immediately swam over and accompanied the CURV, aiming his camera down on it from above.

The other diver spotted Mark sliding through the water from the other direction, and fixed his lens on him.

Mark probed the bottom, his head turning from

side to side. While air bubbles churned up from the two divers, none came from Mark.

Mark and the CURV found their respective torpedoes quickly. Separated by fifty yards under their buoys, the two dummy bombs were partly sunk in the mud.

The CURV positioned itself near one torpedo, and slowly extended its claw toward it. There was a dull *thunk* as the claw banged onto the top of it, withdrew a few feet, came in again, got a tenuous grip on it, began to lift, and then dropped it. Two more times the claw moved into the torpedo before it got a hold firm enough to begin tugging it free from the mud.

Mark, meanwhile, had dropped straight down beside his torpedo, anchored his feet in the mud, locked his arms around the torpedo, yanked it quickly free, and immediately headed for the surface with the bomb in tow.

Mark broke the surface with his torpedo just as the CURV was moving in for its third try at a grip on its sunken prey.

Elizabeth and the admiral watched stunned through their binoculars as Mark surged through the water toward the buoy tender, pushing his torpedo ahead of him like a surfboard.

"He did it!" she exclaimed softly.

"Wow!" said Lt. Ainsley.

Admiral Pierce slowly lowered his binoculars and shook his head, grinning in wonder.

Mark easily deposited his torpedo in the net slung over the side of the ship, and turned back to look toward the buoys.

The water around the buoys was boiling, which indicated that the CURV was still at work below.

Mark looked up at Elizabeth, who bent over the railing above him, then looked back at the buoys.

"No, Mark," she said. "It's fine. You were perfect. Let the CURV finish its work without you."

Mark did several somersaults in the water, then idly floated around on his back.

The ensign appeared at Admiral Pierce's side. "CURV signals indicate substantial progress on recovery, sir. Estimate surfacing in five minutes."

The admiral ignored him and walked over to Elizabeth. "Very impressive, Doctor. Let's get him in and put him under pressure while we're waiting for the films."

In the Research Control Room, Elizabeth sat before a bank of monitors and controls and handles and gauges. Admiral Pierce stood behind her, Ainsley to the side.

Through the circular port they could see the inside of the Pressure Test Tank. At the bottom of the tank, three drums of different sizes were secured by chains. Paint-stenciled on the side of one was the legend "18,000 FT (8,810 psi)"; on the second, "24,000 FT (10,680 psi)"; and on the third drum, "30,000 FT (13,350 psi)."

From the control room, the tank could be put under various pressures, simulating the depths marked on the drums.

Mark appeared swimming above the drums.

Admiral Pierce nodded. "All right, take him down."

Elizabeth spoke into a microphone. "Mark, we're putting you under pressure."

She began to turn dials, keeping an eye on the digital depth gauges, whose numbers ascended furiously. "He's at fifteen thousand feet, sir."

"Take him to twenty."

"Mark," she said into the mike, noting through the port that he was swimming around comfortably, "we're taking you down to twenty thousand feet."

She moved the dials and watched as the depth gauges registered "16,000, 17,000 . . ."

Mark seemed unaffected by the pressure. He undulated evenly, circling the drums.

The numbers on the depth gauges flashed by in front of Elizabeth. Suddenly something happened in the tank. The first drum, marked "18,000 FT," bent inward and collapsed. The three faces in the control room stared at the gauges, which continued to record the increased pressure.

Finally the numbers stopped.

"Twenty thousand feet," Elizabeth announced calmly.

They watched through the port as Mark looked down at the crushed drum, then continued swimming around.

"Take him to thirty," said the admiral.

"Taking you to thirty thousand feet, Mark."

She spun the dials, and the numbers of the gauges flitted by faster and faster.

"Twenty-five thousand feet," Elizabeth said, her voice a bit taut.

The second drum bent and collapsed. Mark hovered near it for a moment, watching it curiously.

"Thirty thousand feet and holding." Elizabeth set the dials, and saw that the depth gauges stayed fixed.

As they watched, the last drum began to bend and flatten like a tin can under a heel. Mark swam around it, observing, while its sides flexed inward until it was entirely collapsed.

"Holy Moses," gasped Lt. Ainsley.

"He seems to be as comfortable at thirty thousand as at five," the admiral said. "All your backup gauges confirm?"

"Yes sir." She motioned along the controls. "All at thirty. And of course the drums were inspected just before the test."

"And he needs no decompression."

"No sir. He'll come right up, whenever I say."

"Or he could stay down a while."

"He could stay down there a month, Admiral, if there was food in there."

"It appears he could go even deeper, if required."

"There are hardly any places that *are* deeper, Admiral. But it seems that depth makes no difference at all to him."

"All right. Bring him up. I'm convinced. What a find for the Navy."

"Yes sir," she said, a bit somberly.

## chapter 4

"Of course I haven't been avoiding you, Doug. I've just been so busy with this project."

They sat in his car at the edge of the bluff, watching the sun sink beyond the Pacific.

"So now are you about finished with it, or what?"

She had told him nothing of what she was doing, except that it involved the mysterious man Doug had seen at the hospital, and confirming what she had done with him in the surf to revive him, and why.

"I don't know if I'll ever be finished, Doug, exactly. I mean, there are still so many things about him we don't know. But at least we've run him through all the major tests at least once, so we're both taking a couple of days off."

"And it turns out that he actually has gills?"

"Something like that."

"What caused you to suddenly be so sure, back there in the beginning, at the hospital?"

She wrinkled her brow and pursed her lips. "I don't know for certain. I wasn't really sure so much as desperate. It just kind of hit me, at the time. I suppose if I'd been a practicing medical doctor, like you, dealing with human beings all the time, it never would have occurred to me. But I've been working with sea animals, and gills. Even as it was, I don't remember it as being anything like a rational deduction. It was just a flash. I'm surprised you didn't see a light bulb over my head."

"I had an interesting time explaining that whole business to the hospital staff."

"How'd you do it?"

He shrugged. "Around here, you can go a long way just saying 'Navy business.' I don't suppose that convinced our bright young resident, Dr. Bock. But fortunately he's neither nosy nor rumor-prone." He turned to her. "You look tired, Elizabeth."

"I am, I guess. Sorry it shows."

"You work too much. A young woman like you ought to be enjoying herself more."

"I am enjoying myself, Doug—immensely, in fact. What I'm doing is terribly satisfying. And anyway, you work just as much as I do."

"Ah, you know how it is, at the hospital. Always something. But at least I try to manage some free time, for pleasure and relaxation."

"From what you've told me about your two former wives, they seemed to feel you were entirely too involved in your work."

"That's how they felt, I guess."

"Well, you and I are about the same in that regard, Doug. That's why neither of us would make good marriage partners just now."

"I wasn't proposing."

She laughed lightly and put a hand on his arm. "No. Not this time you weren't." She turned and stared out the windshield. "Sure is a big ocean out there."

"Yeah. I'd love to be out on it, on a yacht. Trouble with you is, you'd rather be out there *under* it, breathing canned air and communicating with sharks."

"Sometime, I promise you, I'm going to get you into scuba gear and you're going to try it. It's so awesomely beautiful, especially around the reefs."

"I got sinus trouble."

"You don't have to go deep. The most beautiful diving is near the surface, where you have some light from the sun filtering through."

"Claustrophobia is what I'd have. I couldn't stand a mask over my face."

"Except a surgical one, right? I'd get claustrophobia in the operating room every day, under those hot lights, with everybody crowding around and mumbling."

"It's a living."

"You love it."

"Yes, Elizabeth," he sighed and tapped the steering wheel, "I guess I do. Just like you love your work. All our love is poured into our work."

"Not all, silly. We're not automatons. And not forever. My feeling is, you can't schedule your loves like operations. They come when they come, go when they go, change when they change. I wouldn't want you to disappear from my life."

"Oh, don't worry. I'll be around here, creaking and wheezing, when I'm seventy-five, waiting to take you to lunch."

"Speaking of lunch, thank you. It was a treat not having tuna fish from the Navy mess for once."

"You're welcome. Maybe we ought to switch to kelp, like your Mark there. Can you imagine that diet every day? Without French fries? Without gin? Without butter-pecan ice cream?"

"No. But he thrives."

"Yeah. By the way, what've you got lined up for him? Seems to me that he ought to be joining the ranks of the gainfully employed pretty soon."

"Nothing yet. But I'm sure the Navy will find something for him. They can't stand to have any able bodies around without having them do *something*, even if it's pointless."

"He'd be great at scraping bottom paint. They wouldn't even need a dry dock."

"I hope it'll be something better than that."

"Well, let me know when he gets a job. We'll celebrate."

"I hope so. I really hope we can."

Elizabeth was watching again the divers' films of Mark and the CURV recovering their torpedoes, when there was a knock on her office door. She opened it, and Lt. Ainsley stood before her.

"Dr. Merrill, Admiral Pierce would like to see you right away. He has a job for your fish."

She stiffened. "His name is Mark Harris, and he isn't a—"

"Would you come with me, please?"

She followed him.

The admiral's office was a spacious room with a floor-to-ceiling window wall looking out on the ship channel. Pictures and models of various submarines hung on the walls. The admiral sat behind his broad desk examining a sheaf of papers.

Lt. Ainsley knocked and then opened the door and ushered Elizabeth in.

The admiral looked up quickly. "Dr. Merrill. Come in. Have a seat." He pressed buttons on his desk. Over the door red letters lit up: "THIS MEETING IS . . . CLOSED . . . SECRET . . . RECORDED."

The lieutenant closed the door behind them. The admiral motioned to the plush, black leather armchair facing his desk. Elizabeth sat down. The lieutenant remained standing at the door.

Elizabeth leaned forward in her seat. "The lieutenant said you—"

"We'll get right to the point, Doctor." His voice was firm. "Two weeks ago we lost the *Sea Quest* at the bottom of the Mariana Trench . . ."

Elizabeth blanched.

". . . I need your man to find it and help us recover it with the bodies of the crew."

"Did you say the *Sea Quest*?"

The admiral looked past her at Ainsley. "She wasn't told?"

"No sir."

"I assumed you were informed, Doctor. In any event . . ."

"With Commander Roth?" Unconsciously she rose partway from her chair.

"Yes. You knew him? . . . Of course. Similar line of work. Perhaps you'd like to sit down, Doctor." He motioned calmly again to the chair.

She sat down quickly. "I'm fine. Just surprised, naturally." She paused a moment, took a breath, then said evenly, "You were saying, Admiral, that the *Sea Quest* went down in the Mariana Trench."

"Yes." He studied her, appreciating her toughness and professionalism. "It will be a tremendously important mission, which I believe your man can accomplish. Others might not think so, of course, but then they don't know what I—what we—know, do they?"

"No sir."

"In any event, your man has the best chance of success of anyone, or anything, I know. It will be a secret mission with an appropriate cover. By the way," he tapped a thick file on his desk, "all information concerning your work—which we have named 'Project: Atlantis'—will remain classified. Better for us and safer for him. You never know who might want to get their paws on him."

"If I may, sir, what happened to the *Sea Quest*?"

"Went to lay down a package of seismic probes, and just fell off the scope at thirty-six thousand feet. No S.O.S., no message, no nothing." He looked at the wall. "Most advanced technology we own—one of a kind and it's gone."

"And you lost a good crew, too."

"Of course. Of course. I hope you know that I care about them as well."

She nodded slowly. "Surely you've tried to locate it."

"Oh yes . . ." He rose and walked over to stare out the window. He watched some seamen tie up a small research vessel that had just come in. ". . . Yes indeed. Sent down a lot of expensive hardware, but we still haven't found it. That is, we can safely assume it lies somewhere directly beneath where we last had a fix on it. But we haven't been able to pick it up on our sensors. It's crucial that we find it first."

"First?"

"Before, you know, anybody else . . ." His voice trailed off. He turned to look at her.

"But who else could . . ."

"Doctor, we don't know precisely what every nation's underwater capabilities are. We do know that the other side has performed some highly successful and impressive deep-water probes. Surely you can understand how valuable it is for us to keep *Sea Quest* out of foreign hands. Some of our most sophisticated apparatus was on that vessel. The crew is lost. I don't mean to be hardhearted about that. But there's nothing we can do to bring them back alive. It is in the interests of protecting other lives that we must recover *Sea Quest.*"

She narrowed her eyes and stared at him. "I understand."

"We've tried everything else. So we're going to have to use your man to get a handle on it quickly. If he can find it, he can hitch our recovery cables to it."

"I see."

"We will take all necessary precautions—both for him and for us. He'll be under escort when he's in the water—for as far down as possible. And he'll be tethered always, for, uh, security's sake."

Color returned to Elizabeth's face. She set her jaw firmly. "I'm sorry, Admiral," she said quietly, "but Mark Harris is not just a piece of hardware."

"No, of course not."

"And I don't think you should think of him either as some expendable trained animal."

"No, not at all . . ."

"He is sensitive to personalities and directions."

"Doctor, I know that," he said calmly, leaning across the desk toward her. "I am aware of his sensibilities and loyalty and performance, thanks to you. I know he responds to you. That's why I'm asking you to handle him for me."

Elizabeth averted her eyes to gaze out the window. She pondered his words. The admiral was quiet, allowing her to think. Slowly she turned back to him. "Admiral, for the sake of the whole situation all the way around, I think it would be best if you made your request to Mark directly."

They studied each other.

After a moment, the admiral nodded. "All right, I'll talk to him. But why me?"

"I think you have to make it clear that this job comes from you, not me."

"Why?"

"Because this job might not . . . be successful."

"Doctor," his voice was quiet but firm, "I think I understand your feelings."

"It's not just my *feelings*, Admiral. It's my knowledge about Mark. And my *lack* of knowledge. We don't know for sure what the outer limits of his abilities are. But in any case he will perform better if he understands just what's involved. Then he will be willing to look to me for guidance and support."

"You're willing, then, to oversee the mission?"

"Of course," she said icily. "Mark Harris is my job."

"But you wish for me to go alone to tell him?"

"Without me, at least. It'll be less confusing to him. When I give him an assignment, he expects me to be able to explain it fully, every detail. That will not be possible in this case."

"As you wish. I respect your judgment."

The sign on the fence said: RESTRICTED AREA—AUTHORIZED PERSONNEL ONLY.

Lt. Ainsley slowed the car as they approached the

gate where two armed guards were posted. The guards stepped to either side of the car, stooped to look in, and quickly waved it through.

They pulled up near the dolphin pool and walked over. Two more armed guards were now posted around the pool.

"Quite efficient, Ainsley," the admiral said, gesturing toward the guards.

"Thank you, sir."

"Although I don't know why you weren't able to get things straightened out with him this morning."

"Sorry, sir. I tried."

They looked down into the pool.

Mark lay resting at the bottom. His eyes were closed. As the two shadows fell on the water, he opened them. He lay unmoving, staring up.

Ainsley leaned over. "Hey," he called. Mark didn't move. Ainsley cupped his hands around his mouth. "Hey, there! You! Mark Harris! We want to talk to you again!"

After a few moments, Mark rolled lazily over and began swimming in a slow upward spiral. He broke the surface a few feet from the edge and looked at the two men.

"Look here," Ainsley said in a slow, loud voice, as if Mark were partly deaf, "you know who this is?" He hooked a thumb toward the admiral. "*This is the—*"

"It's okay, Ainsley," the admiral broke in, tapping him on the shoulder. "Mark, Lt. Ainsley here tells me you didn't seem to understand my orders when he delivered them to you a little while ago. What didn't you understand, son?"

Mark started moving slowly around the pool like a lazy eel.

"He can't answer you, sir. He can't talk."

"I know, I know." The admiral walked alongside where Mark was swimming. "Mark, the orders were fairly simple." Mark swam away.

The admiral turned to Ainsley. "What exactly did you tell him?"

"Just what you said, sir. All about the mission."

"And you told him you were acting in Dr. Merrill's behalf?"

"Well, I told him she had talked to you. And that you had told me to deliver your orders. And I told him these were your orders."

"Darn it, Ainsley! That's the most confusing thing I ever heard! It was supposed to be simple. The whole point was that he is supposed to understand that Dr. Merrill told you to talk to him!"

"Well, I just figured, unh, you know, the proper authority for . . ."

"Proper authority in this case, as far as Mark Harris is concerned, is Dr. Merrill! You know what the arrangement was!"

"Yes sir." The lieutenant blushed and looked down at the grass. "I guess I just got confused myself. Because as I understood, the arrangement was for *you* to talk to him."

The admiral sighed, puffed out his chest and let it relax. "Okay, okay. I just thought you could save me some time by giving him an initial briefing. I should have done it just like she said."

"It might not have made any difference, sir. He just wasn't responsive at all. Didn't even pay attention."

"Maybe." He turned his attention back to the pool where Mark was swimming in lazy circles. "Son, let me explain it to you again. Dr. Merrill knows I am here. She asked me to talk to you about this. Wednesday—that's two days from now—you leave on a ship. Not so much different from the one you were on the other day, just bigger and more comfortable. Dr. Merrill will be with you on the ship. Then you go down into the ocean to help us find a piece of equipment we've lost. Just like the torpedo the other day. Except that you don't even have to bring it back this time. Just find it and we'll do the rest. Understand? Do you understand that?"

Mark stopped swimming and straightened up in the water. He looked at the admiral, indicating neither yes nor no—just a cool, appraising look.

The admiral rubbed his eyes and crouched next to the water. "Perhaps I'd better explain it to you a little differently. You see, we don't have anybody, or anything, that can find this piece of equipment. It's terribly important equipment. A kind of boat. We have to get it back. You're the only one who can do it."

Mark began circling again.

The admiral got down on all fours and leaned over the pool. "Look, son, this is one of the most important things Dr. Merrill has ever done. It's not, it isn't just—it's more than machinery, son. There are people inside. Yes, that's it," he nodded briskly, "two people. Friends of Dr. Merrill."

Mark surfaced near the admiral and peered at him.

The admiral spoke more quickly. "And these friends of Dr. Merrill, we want to get them back too. You understand? Of course you do. So if you go down there, you can find the equipment *and* the people. Why don't you come out of the pool so we can talk about it?"

Mark swam over to the ladder and climbed out.

"Don't you think you ought to tell him they'll be *bodies*, sir?" Ainsley whispered. "What if he gets down there and finds out that they're—"

"I just want him out of the pool, Ainsley. Once we get him working with Dr. Merrill, it'll be all right."

Mark walked around to them, and the three moved over to a gentle rise on the Center grounds. The admiral sat down and Mark joined him a few feet away on the slope. Mark glanced into the sun and quickly rubbed his eyes.

"Run inside and get his sunglasses, Ainsley."

Below them in the ship channel several vessels were moored. Work crews busily loaded some, unloaded others. Trucks came and went. The water sparkled in the sun. Beyond the channel, the vast Pacific shone like a mirror.

Ainsley returned with the glasses and Mark slipped them on. He looked out across the water.

"Son," the admiral began softly, "there are some things about this place, and us, that are difficult for you to understand. This entire country, for as far east as you can see and more, is run by a government that oversees everything. Protects us all. I work for the government. Right now, with you here, everything on this base is my responsibility. I look after it for the government and the people. There are other people in other countries who do not like us, who would like to harm us. I help defend the country against those people."

Mark continued staring down the hillside.

"Now, somebody has to be the leader, the boss. Do you understand that? Somebody has to tell others what to do. Usually people will agree to do what they are told, because they trust the boss. But sometimes they don't completely understand why they are being told to do something. Or sometimes they don't want to do it, even when they should. So we have orders. When the boss in the Navy gives orders, it means you have to obey. I give orders." He took a breath. "Orders are when . . ."

Mark leaned forward, staring at the docks and the water.

". . . when people older and wiser tell us what to do. And then we do it. We must do it. That's how we get things done." He leaned around to try to get Mark's attention. "We get things done by obeying orders. Otherwise important jobs would take forever. You follow me, son? Hunh? Am I getting through to you? Obeying orders is what it's all about."

Mark gave him a sharp, questioning look.

"See? Now you're getting it. Now you're beginning to understand." He reached out to tap Mark's shoulder. Mark looked down at the hand. "And as long as you're here, you'll have to obey my orders too. Because I am older and wiser. You will have to do what I tell you to do. You understand?"

Mark looked steadily at the admiral, his penetrating, green-eyed gaze causing the admiral to shift his position nervously.

"Now then. Here's what I order you to . . . Hey!"

Mark had stood up, and was now walking briskly down the grassy hill straight toward the ship channel.

"Hey there! You better not walk away like this when I'm giving you an order!"

Mark continued walking.

"Ainsley!"

"Yes sir! I'll get him, sir!"

Ainsley trotted down the slope after Mark, waving his finger in the air. "Stop! I order you to stop!"

Two MP's at the gate, hearing the commands, swung around to block Mark's path.

Mark charged forward and burst between them, running toward the dock.

"Keep him out of the water!" Ainsley screamed.

"What?" The guards looked at him.

"Everybody! Don't let him dive!"

Two more MP's jumped out of a dockside jeep between Mark and the channel.

Mark cut to his left and ran onto the road. Whistles were blown, MP's materialized all around.

Mark darted behind a row of forklifts, reversed his direction, cut behind a jeep, and headed back up the road the other way.

The admiral stood on the grass, dancing on one foot and then the other, breathing heavily.

Mark ran at the fence, tried to climb it, fell back coughing. He lurched toward the channel. An MP got a hand on him and spun him around into the grasp of another.

"We got him!" they called.

Mark swung his body furiously, breaking free. Coughing and gasping and stumbling, he ran along the channel past the ships. In the distance before him lay the open Pacific. He lost his footing on the oil-slicked pavement and tumbled. He scratched his way forward, regaining his footing as he moved.

"Don't let him get to the water!" Ainsley bellowed.

They were right behind him. The Pacific lay before him, a few yards away.

An MP made a diving tackle from the rear. Mark

continued to advance, dragging the MP behind with his right leg. He reached out for the water.

Then several other MP's pounced on top of him, and he collapsed. He lay face down, breathing in shallow gasps, his outstretched arm three feet from the water's edge.

Though he lay helpless, the MP's didn't know that, and they grabbed frantically for various holds, hammerlocks, and half nelsons. Most of their struggle was with each other as they bumped, butted, and kicked.

The admiral raced out the gate and down the road to where they all lay in a snaky tangle. "Take it easy! Don't hurt him! Take it easy!"

"We didn't let him get to the water, sir!" Ainsley announced proudly, snapping to attention.

"Okay, okay! Get off him now, come on!" The admiral reached down and began pulling MP's off Mark. "Ease up now. He's not dangerous. Come on, just two of you guys lift him up and take his arms."

Gradually they untangled and lifted Mark up.

He could barely stand. The admiral was gratified to see that despite the pileup, Mark didn't seem to be injured. But he could also see that he was exhausted and dangerously out of his element.

"Quickly now," he waved the men toward the lab, "get him into the pool!"

"But I thought the lieutenant said—"

"Into the pool! On the double!"

The admiral, Ainsley, and two MP's hauled Mark—as quickly and gently as they could—away through the gate and toward the pool.

The other MP's watched, scratching their helmets. "What was that all about?"

"Beats me. For a guy that looks strong, he sure went down easy."

"Yeah, but what did the guy do?"

"Goin' AWOL, I guess."

"Since when they put you in the pool for goin' AWOL?"

"Maybe he was tryin' to commit suicide in the ocean."

"So they gonna let him do it in the darn *pool*?"

"Maybe he was gonna swim to Japan."

"Anyway, we did what we were supposed to do. We gotta make out a report?"

"Not unless they tell us to, we ain't."

"He's right. Our orders were to stop him, that's all."

"And that we done, first class!"

Mark swam swiftly around and around the pool, occasionally splashing the water angrily. Two MP's watched him, drawing back from the splashes, which seemed to come most often when he was near them.

Elizabeth trotted out from her office to the pool and dropped to her knees. "Mark!"

He stopped briefly, then resumed swimming fiercely around.

"Mark! Please! Listen to me!"

He kept swimming and splashing the MP's. She waited patiently. He didn't splash her. Gradually his pace slowed. He dove for the bottom and lay there, staring up.

Elizabeth looked down into the water at him.

"Thank the Lord he stopped wettin' us down," an MP muttered.

For several minutes Mark lay on the bottom, his hands behind his head like a pillow. Elizabeth didn't move from her knees. She kept looking at him.

Finally she turned to the MP's, who were shaking the wet out of their pants legs. "Listen, men, I want you to back off for a while, okay? On my authority. Just move back away from the pool a few yards while I try to talk to him."

They looked at her suspiciously. Then one of them shrugged. "Okay, let's do like she says. She's the doctor. He's gotta come up soon anyway. For a guy who can't fight a lick, he sure can hold his breath when he's mad." They moved away onto the grass.

"Mark? Will you listen to me?" She leaned out over the water so that if he couldn't hear her he could see her lips move.

Gradually he moved from where he'd been reclining and circled up to the surface at the center of the pool. He stared at her.

"Mark, I don't know exactly what you were told, and I don't know exactly what happened. Somebody made a mistake. There's nothing I can do about that. But maybe we can just start over with this whole thing."

He floated nearly still at the center of the pool, only his head out of the water, his green eyes glowing.

"Mark, the admiral came to see me yesterday. He wanted some help from you and me. He wanted to know if you will help him recover the submarine. As a favor to him, Mark. Not an order—a favor."

She met his cold gaze and bit her lip lightly. "And he wants us to work together, Mark. You and me. That's what he came to see you about. I guess it all got misunderstood somehow. The admiral is a good man. He really is. When you tried to leave, he sent those men after you because you're just too valuable for him to lose. He didn't know how to stop you otherwise. He didn't want you hurt. You didn't get hurt, did you?"

She paused, as if expecting him to answer. "And Mark, I would like you to stay here too. I would hate to see you leave. There is so much I want to learn about you—want you to learn about me, about us. So I want you to stay. But not like this. Not with force. That will not happen again. I hope you will stay with us because you want to. You understand?"

He continued to stare at her. She studied his face. She thought she could detect a softening. Nothing anybody else could detect, probably. Maybe there was no change. But she thought his unblinking eyes flashed a bit less angrily.

"Mark, I will not desert you. Do you understand that? I will never lie to you. I will stay with you so long as you are here. I will not give you orders. I will ask you to do things, and you will do them if you want to—just like before. Understand? Now, it was a mistake, what happened with the admiral. He feels very badly about it. He would tell you that himself, but he is afraid that if he comes out here it will make you angry again. So he wants me to be with you when he talks to you from now on."

Gradually Mark moved closer to her.

"So listen, Mark. I'm going to try to work something out with the admiral. We will reach an agreement about that mission, the three of us. You will agree only if you want to. And then we will stick to that agreement."

Mark was near the edge of the pool.

"Will you trust me?"

Slowly he reached up and touched her outstretched hand.

The admiral sat behind his broad desk. He swiveled back and forth in a slow arc. His eyes were narrowed in concentration. His hands were pressed together to form a steeple, his thumbs against his chin, his index fingers against the tip of his nose.

Elizabeth sat in an armchair facing the desk. She was dressed in white pants and smock. Her left leg was crossed over her right, her hands primly stacked on her left knee.

Mark stood with his back to them, staring out at the ship channel. He was wearing blue Navy work denims, and dark glasses.

They were the only ones in the room. Over the door the SECRET sign was lit.

Finally the admiral spoke. "You are suggesting a very hard bargain, Dr. Merrill. I sense you feel you have me at a disadvantage, and mean to make full use of it."

"No sir," she said calmly. "I just think that you are asking an awful lot from Mark. He deserves something of equal value in return. What I am requesting in his behalf is the only thing I know of that I believe he wants very much. It's a way for both of you to get what you want. Mark finds your sub. You let him go home."

He stopped swiveling and leaned forward over the desk on his forearms. "Doctor, if he's suffering from amnesia as you reported, going home seems an unlikely possibility. After all, he must have got terribly lost and confused to end up on our shores near death.

To send him back now might be akin to releasing to the jungle an ape raised in captivity. Don't you fear for his survival?"

Elizabeth glanced uncomfortably over at Mark, who remained motionless with his back to them, looking out the window. "Medical science can't determine the duration of his amnesia, Admiral. It may be only a recent occurrence that wouldn't interfere with his basic experience and instincts. No, I wouldn't worry about him returning to the sea."

"And what if it didn't work? What if he ended up washed back up on the beach just like before?"

"I would hope, Admiral, that if he ever returned, he would always be welcome here."

"Doctor, this is the Navy! This isn't some mission where the misfits of the world can drift in and out for meals and showers whenever they please!"

He leaned back, huffing, his face flushed. Gradually he relaxed. "Sorry. Forgive my outburst."

"In any event, Admiral," she went on calmly, "one thing is certain. Mark wants to return to the ocean. He wants to be free."

"And in this particular instance we're dealing with here, he wants to go on this mission with no tether line."

"I'm sure he won't go into the water with it."

"Not even for his own safety?"

"No. You'll just have to trust him."

"And with just one supervisor to whom he is responsible—you."

"You'll have to trust me also. And I'm the only one he trusts. That must be quite clear to you—now."

For a long moment, neither of them spoke. They averted their eyes from each other.

Then the admiral addressed her quietly. "Doctor, you'd better be right. For both our sakes."

They locked eyes for a moment. Then the admiral snapped open a file in front of him and took out a sheaf of documents. He spread a series of pictures across the desk. "This is the sub that's down."

Elizabeth rose and stepped to the desk. "Mark?" He turned, and she motioned him over. "These are the pictures of what you'll be looking for."

Mark stared down at the pictures of the *Sea Quest*, an odd-looking acrylic globe on catamaran skids, with various arms, sensors, ports, lights, and cameras visible on the outside. His eyes shifted slightly to the pictures of the two-man crew: standing at attention, leaning against the sub, crouching together and smiling at the camera. He stared closely at each picture on the desk before moving to the next, as if committing their details to memory.

Then he looked up at the admiral.

"These were the two men on board, Commanders Philip Roth and David Hendricks. You find us this sub and the bodies of the men . . ."

Mark glanced quickly at Elizabeth.

". . . and I'll consider your request."

Elizabeth tensed. "It's not a request, Admiral. It's a deal or the whole thing's . . ."

"Yes, Doctor?" He smiled faintly.

She clenched her fists and her voice exploded: "This man has a name! Mark Harris! And he has rights! Just like—"

"I know his name," the admiral's voice rose too, "and I know his rights! He has whatever rights I say he has! And I don't need any rudder orders from you!"

His big fist thumped down on his desk. They glared at each other.

Then Mark's hand came down firmly to cover the admiral's fist.

The admiral looked up, startled.

Mark's other hand came down softly on Elizabeth's shoulder.

"Yes." Mark's voice stunned them. "I say yes to the admiral."

They could only gape as he spoke for the first time.

Mark nodded slowly and looked at each of them in turn, his face impassive, his hands on them with gentle firmness. "I say yes."

The room fell silent. Mark shifted his left hand from the admiral's fist up to his shoulder, and he applied soft, insistent pressure to both him and Elizabeth, guiding them back into their seats. He looked at the pictures on the desk.

"I will find your *Sea Quest*. And your . . . bodies."

## chapter 5

Given their knowledge that he had fully developed vocal cords, that Mark suddenly spoke was not as curious as why he had not spoken before. But whenever Elizabeth questioned him about it, he just shook his head.

Still, his speaking now was of enormous assistance in their hurrying ahead with preparations for the mission. That he could make statements and reply to questions cut the time it took to deal with him in half. He spoke simply and seldom. He was not one for chitchat. He responded when asked something, asked questions himself when necessary, or offered brief comments when appropriate.

It was early evening when the small, blue Navy minibus carrying Mark and Elizabeth and their equipment pulled up near the USS *Moon River*, a World War II submarine tender converted to scientific use, moored at the dock.

The deck of the gray ship was alive with seamen at work among the thick cables anking in and out of the diving well's open hatches, with men manning lines and davits and cranks and hammers and wrenches. The air was filled with hammering and hollering and creaking as preparations were completed. Men walked up the gangplank laden with gear and returned to the dock empty-handed for additional equipment.

Elizabeth and Mark approached the gangplank, stood aside while a row of men passed, then walked up and stepped onto the deck.

One of the men who was seated on the deck working with wrenches on some diving gear looked up. He was broad-built and sturdy, with a square face and square hands, and dark, curly hair. He wiped his oil-smeared hands on a rag, rose to his feet, and he walked over to them. Still wiping his hands, he smiled broadly and said, "How you doin'? One of you must be Dr. Merrill."

Elizabeth smiled back. "I'm Dr. Merrill. This is Mark Harris."

The man stuck out his hand, then quickly pulled it back and wiped some more. "Glad to meet you. I'm the master diver, Ernie Davis. Welcome aboard."

"Thank you."

Mark looked around curiously, his eyes hidden behind dark glasses.

"Well, Doctor, you runnin' the show?"

"That's right, Mr. Davis."

"Good deal. That's just fine." He cocked his head to look at her, then shook it slightly. "Just fine. Let me take you to the OIC, Mr. Johnson."

He led them past bunches of sailors absorbed in their preparations, around some coiled hawsers, under networks of electronic wires, to a calmer part of the deck where Lieutenant Commander Arnie Johnson stood.

Davis made the introductions as the ship's commander scrutinized the pair.

"Well, let's see what we have here," Johnson said. "As I understand it, Ernie will take Mr. Harris down on the platform, and he'll go in at two hundred feet." He looked at Mark. "What sort of rig are you using?"

"Mr. Harris will be testing some new equipment," Elizabeth put in quickly. "A re-breathing turtle pack with a self-heating luralite suit."

"That so? Well, somebody's gotta test the new stuff. As for us, we still like our old Kirby-Morgans. Maybe we're a little old-fashioned there. But we don't have much time for testing. We're working all the time, so our stuff's gotta be tried and true. Old Kirby-Morgans. Right, Chief?"

Ernie Davis nodded. "Keeps us from getting our tails caught in the cracks."

"You have tails?"

All eyes quickly turned toward Mark.

Ernie reflected Mark's deadpan delivery. "I got 'em the same time they put in the gills."

"I see." Mark nodded.

Davis smiled. Johnson continued to stare uncertainly at Mark.

"These divers and their jokes," Elizabeth said, forcing a slight smile.

Johnson looked at her. "By the way, Doctor, my orders show that Mr. Harris will not be using a tether line. I take it that's not a joke."

"Correct."

He looked back at Mark. "Nobody steps off that platform at two hundred feet without a tether."

"Well, Mr. Harris does," Elizabeth's voice became firmer, "in this case. This new equipment requires exceptional freedom."

"Freedom's fine, but at that depth we—"

"So that's the way it'll be. We'll all just follow the orders that you received. Are there any other problems?"

"All right." Commander Johnson rubbed the back of his neck. "But you know the area you'll be running your tests is close by the spot where the *Sea Quest* went down."

"We know."

"And where the Russian research sub was lost last year."

"No, we didn't—"

"And the French sub went down there the year before. It's a dangerous part of the world."

Mark and the commander studied each other.

Elizabeth scuffed one toe on the deck. She gave the commander a warm smile. "I'm sure with your ship up top, Mr. Harris will be fine."

"Well, there's not much we can do if he gets lost or tangled up down there, without a tether."

"We understand."

"I will be fine," Mark said.

"Mr. Davis will show you to your quarters. We cast off in an hour."

The commander spun on his heel and walked off.

Elizabeth carefully stowed her gear. Then she washed her face, combed her hair, and put on a small amount of makeup. She sat on the edge of the bunk and stared at the wall. She soon became aware of faint groans in the hull as the ship moved from the dock, and a bit later felt a gentle heave as the ship moved into the open Pacific. She enjoyed the feeling of the ship's movement, as she always did. But this was not a pleasure trip. Not even an ordinary work trip, where she might look forward to diving herself.

This would be the supreme test for Mark Harris—in several ways. She dared hope it would not be the last. That he would not be hurt. That he would not disappear. That it would be successful.

But even success in this case was not a pleasant thought. Success would mean that while finding and recovering the *Sea Quest,* he would also find and recover the body of Phil Roth. Success would be a sad event.

Suddenly she felt very tired. She lay down on the bunk and closed her eyes, and soon the rhythmic rolling of the ship lulled her to sleep.

Mark stared at himself in the morror. He traced the outlines of his face with his fingers, and then ran his palms down the smooth skin of his chest. He took a deep breath and watched his chest expand.

He ran the sink full of water and ducked his head into it. Elizabeth had arranged for a special tub to be installed in a little-used storeroom, and there he would later immerse himself for sleep. But meanwhile the sink would allow him a quick, restorative belt of water. He remained bent over the sink for several minutes, until there was a knock at the door.

He put on his sunglasses and opened the door to see Ernie Davis, who smiled and held up a palm.

"Hi there. Thought you might like to take a little tour of our ship, see what we got on board."

"Yes."

"Come on, grab a shirt. The boss is strict about no bare chests, especially when we got a dame on board."

"A dame." Mark took his shirt off the wall hook and slipped it on.

"Yeah, a looker too, ain't she? You're lucky. I'd love to test some stuff for her. We'll check out the decompression units first, okay?"

"Yes."

They wound through passageways and stooped through bulkheads and finally entered a control room with a large TV monitor.

"This is our deck decompression chamber," Davis said. "Maybe you been in one like it. Deep-diving-system Mark II Mod Zero. Let's see who's on TV."

They stepped to the monitor. It showed in the chamber a big blond man in a loose shirt and swim trunks seated, elbows on his knees, his chin in his hands.

"That is one of your divers," Mark said.

"Yeah, right. Jack Turner. Real deep-diving sucker. Strong as an ox. Little short on judgment," Ernie tapped his head with the point of his finger; "likes to chase sharks around, punch 'em in the nose. But so long as we send him down with somebody stable he's one of our best."

"When he comes back . . . you put him . . . in there."

"Regular decompression, sure. Same routine you're used to." He looked quizzically at Mark.

"Better to have gills, like you."

Ernie narrowed his eyes. "You givin' me the razz?" Then his look brightened and he winked. "Yeah, you got me, all right. Superdiver like you, I guess you got the right to razz me. I'm just a working stiff. Let's grab a cup of java."

Three divers, two still in wet suits, were sitting at one galley table drinking coffee and bantering. They waved at Ernie when he stepped in.

Ernie walked over, Mark right behind him. "Hey, Popeye, where's the five you owe me?"

One of the wet-suited divers banged his mug down. "Where's the broad you owe *me*, you yo-yo?"

"Jam it, Popeye. Wait'll you get a look at this guy's boss." He turned to Mark. "This is Popeye. He's big as a bear and almost twice as smart." He laughed. "Popeye, this is Mark Harris. Civilian diver."

They all said hello and nodded greetings. Mark nodded back.

Ernie guided Mark into a seat, shoved a mug in front of him, and filled it with coffee from a round silver pot. "Old Mark here, he's gonna walk off the stage over by Harmony Ridge." He slapped him on the back. "He's real good with the razz. Cream and sugar?"

Mark lifted the mug and smelled it. He put it back down on the table.

Popeye slid over beside Ernie. "Harmony Ridge. Ain't that where we got those funny solar blips? Remember?"

The other divers leaned forward over the table.

"Yeah, that's right," one of them said. "The signals."

"Those weird signals," Popeye said. "Just for a while. Then nothin'."

"Yeah, and just that one time. For a few minutes. Never could figure it out."

"You got any ideas on it, Ernie?"

"Sure. Sea monsters."

"Probably. Big old jobs like they got in Loch Ness."

"No." Heads turned toward Mark. "There are no sea monsters in the place you call 'the trench.' "

Ernie shrugged. "Thirty-six thousand feet down. Who could know?"

"I know." Mark looked at Ernie through his sunglasses. "I have been there."

There was an uncomfortable silence while the divers looked at their mugs. Then Ernie chuckled. He slapped Mark on the back. The other divers joined in the laughter.

"See why I like him?" Ernie said. "He catches you that way. Sucks you right in. He's all right."

"What you goin' down after?" one of the divers asked Mark.

"Testing. Equipment."

"What kind?"

Mark looked at him silently.

"I don't think he's supposed to talk about it," Ernie said. "Some secret re-breathing garbage."

"Down there?" The diver shook his head. "Wow."

"Well, I guess we should be movin' on, Mark." Ernie stood up. "Don't blame you for passing on the coffee. That's another thing we're old-fashioned about on this ship—old Navy coffee."

The ship plowed through the dark ocean, churning up a wake that sparkled under the light of a half-moon. The waves swooshed by the sides and the engines rumbled below decks. Wind of the mid-Pacific sang in the rigging and antennae above.

Mark leaned against the railing and stared down into the black sea. He was the only figure on deck until Elizabeth approached from behind and leaned on the railing beside him.

"It's a beautiful night," she said softly, "for me at least." The warm wind tossed her hair and curled it around her face. "I suppose for you it's not as great a pleasure—the moon, the wind, the air—as it is for . . . someone like me."

He stared silently at the steely black swells.

"Are we close to your home, Mark?"

He raised his head slightly to look out across the ocean.

"You still remember nothing about where in the ocean you're from?"

"Perhaps . . . when I am deep in the ocean . . . I will remember."

She was silent for a moment. She pulled a strand of hair out of her eyes and looked at him. "Perhaps when you're deep in the ocean you'll forget that we're up here waiting for you."

"No." His answer was quick and firm.

"Tomorrow, when you dive," she said hesitantly, "when you're very deep, when you're alone in the sea, will that be a pleasure for you?"

"Pleasure?" He turned his head a bit toward her.

"Will you like that?"

For a time he stared out across the water. "I like being in the ocean. It is where there are things that I know. But . . . what I must do . . . is not a pleasure. Your friends . . ."

"Yes." She leaned her head back and looked at the sky. "I'm sorry you must look for them. That is not a pleasure."

"No."

She leaned forward and looked into his face. "Are you afraid?"

"Afraid?"

"I mean, about running into any trouble down there, or . . ." She put a hand on her cheek and shook her head. "No, of course not. Crazy. I keep forgetting what—who you are."

"I am not afraid . . . in the ocean."

"But on land."

"Sometimes. There is much I do not . . . understand. I must always be near the water. It is different with you."

They leaned over the rail and stared out to sea. Elizabeth breathed deeply of the salt air, savoring its fresh tang, yet aware that Mark, standing beside her breathing the same air, was not savoring it. With each breath he took he was nearer the time when he needed to breathe from the water to restore himself. She wondered if he could come to enjoy his times on land as she enjoyed her times down among the reefs.

Elizabeth pinched her lips together, started to speak, hesitated, then turned to him. "Mark, I want you to look at something." From her jacket pocket she took a tiny plastic box. She held it in front of him and snapped it open. In it was a tiny, multifaceted crystal that glittered like a diamond in the moonlight. The crystal was embedded in a foam cushion.

Mark looked at it, then up at Elizabeth.

She plucked it carefully from the box and held it in her palm. "This is a miniature transponder. It sends out signals through the water. Those signals can be picked up by our sensors, here on the ship. We can tell wherever this transponder is in the water, from the signals. Tomorrow, I want you to swallow it . . ." She saw a slight tenseness in his face. "Yes, just swallow it. It won't be difficult. When you swallow it, you won't even know it's inside you. It won't harm you. And it will send out signals. So wherever you go in the ocean we will be able to keep track of you."

She held it out to him. He made no move to take it, just stared at her.

"Please understand, Mark. It's not that we don't trust you. You know how much I trust you. We just want to keep track of you. For your own safety."

Still he looked into her eyes, and did not take it.

"Mark, this transponder will not make you come back. It will not allow anyone to capture you. You will still be free. But if you need help—for any reason—it will let us find you. That's the only reason I want you to take it."

Mark now looked down at the crystal. Gingerly he took it, closing his hand over it.

"Thank you for understanding."

"I do not always understand." Again he gazed out across the night sea. "But I believe you. It is good to be able to believe . . . when you are in a place . . . where you understand . . . so little."

Dawn broke clear on the Pacific over the deepest abyss known to man, the Mariana Trench. At its deepest, the floor lay 35,630 feet below the hull of the U.S.S. *Moon River*.

Preparations for the dive had been going on since before dawn, seamen scurrying over the decks and below them, crane operators moving heavy gear around.

The swells that gently rolled the ship had no effect on the soberly efficient, well-drilled team who worked aboard.

The dive officer and safety officer roamed the deck, watching closely as systems were prepared and checked.

Then, from above, the overhead crane operator signaled that he was ready to lower the dive platform down through the diving well into the sea.

Mark and Ernie emerged from below decks through a hatch. Both wore black wet suits with yellow stripes on the arms and legs. Two assistants assigned to them quickly brought over their equipment and helped Ernie and Mark into diving gear.

Both men had standard breathing regulators attached to flexible hoses that ran to their backpacks, and wide-angle Kirby-Morgan face masks. But their backpacks were not similar. Ernie strapped on a standard set of double air tanks. Mark's apparatus—strange to everyone there except Elizabeth—was a single black square rubber-covered box.

Ernie bit down on his mouthpiece, adjusted it, checked for the passage of air through it. His assistant checked the gauges.

Elizabeth quickly stepped in to take over Mark's final checks. He copied Ernie's moves, and Elizabeth scanned the secretly useless gauges, and nodded.

"All set," she said.

"Ready here," said Ernie's assistant.

Ernie nodded to Mark, and Mark nodded back.

A sailor wearing earmuff headphones leaned his head back and raised his hand, giving the go-ahead signal to the overhead crane operator.

The crane rumbled into action, lowering the dive platform slowly over the dive well. When it was level with the deck, Ernie stepped aboard, assisted by other sailors who watched his arms and feet so they didn't snag anywhere. Then Mark stepped on.

Elizabeth and Mark locked eyes briefly—he peering out through his face mask. Then the platform was lowered into the well and the water, and disappeared from view.

Elizabeth took a deep breath, rubbed her hand over

her eyes, then turned and headed inside for the control station.

Two naval aides, standing at rest with their hands behind their backs, stood at either side of the door when Elizabeth entered. They followed her in, shut the door, and remained standing inside.

She sat quickly on the swivel chair in front of a console with a row of display panels and monitors and microphones. She flicked on several switches, and digital displays lit up in front of her. She activated a tape recorder to one side, then leaned to the other side to flick on the switch that lit up a green scope. A silver dot appeared on the scope.

She spoke into one of the microphones. "Transponder capsule reads five-by-five at 0847 hours. Program for tracking optimum . . ." Her eyes moved back and forth over the readouts. She leaned toward another microphone. "Okay, Ernie, all systems go . . ."

The digital depth gauge read fifteen and descending. On a chart, an electronic writing stylus etched a wavering line. Elizabeth's eyes moved busily over all the gauges and monitors. "All systems go . . ."

Beneath the ship the platform slowly descended, its two passengers standing erect, watching schools of fish flash by. Whatever Ernie did, Mark copied it. When Ernie checked his wrist gauges, Mark did the same. When Ernie adjusted the position of his facemask slightly, or wiped the glass with his mitten, Mark did likewise.

The colors of things in the water began to change. Reds were gone at thirty feet; orange disappeared at thirty-five feet; greens gave way to blue-green tints at eighty; by ninety feet, fish and drifting animals and seaweed all appeared gray-blue.

They stared down into the depths. The first mountainous ridge appeared as a hazy, irregular shape, becoming more distinct as they descended.

Over the mike, Ernie heard faint *pings* coming from Elizabeth's console, then her voice: "You're coming up on one-fifty, one hundred fifty feet . . ."

Sharp canyon walls rose past them in the near distance. Small schools of fish, different sizes but all appearing gray—to Ernie at least—darted by this way and that.

Still they moved slowly down, the only sense of their descent coming from the visions of the canyon walls. That and—again only to Ernie—the increased pressure. Streams of bubbles rose from Ernie's regulator; none came from Mark's.

Again Elizabeth's voice: "You're coming up on two hundred . . . Coming up on two hundred . . . two-oh-oh . . . two hundred . . . Okay, that's it . . . Cable is stopped . . . Okay, men, you're on station . . . All systems still go . . . Clear for your mission . . ."

Ernie checked his wrist gauges, adjusted the regulator in his mouth, leaned over to pat Mark's arm and give him thumbs-up. Then he spoke into his face-mask mike. "Okay, we're hanging loose at two hundred feet. Everything's A-okay down here. We're gonna take a little walk around."

Ernie gestured toward the open water. Mark nodded. Ernie reached around to check the fastenings on his tether rope.

Then Elizabeth's voice came again, unexpectedly:

"Ernie, I have something to explain to you. The special equipment Mark has is more special than we've told you . . ."

Ernie yanked on the rope, testing it.

"It will allow him to go much deeper than anyone knows . . ."

Ernie flexed his shoulders under the straps. "Okay." He tried to disguise the impatience in his voice. To be interrupted with this garbage now, just when he was about to leave the platform, was not wise, and hardly professional. He was concentrating on his equipment and his work. His mind was filled with times and depths. Any minor delays at this depth wasted crucial air time on his tanks.

"Actually, the whole matter is highly classified . . ."

"Then don't tell me," Ernie snapped.

While this conversation was going on, Mark had been behind Ernie, obscured from his vision. He had unstrapped his backpack.

"But Ernie, I must tell you . . ."

"Look, I don't have time to listen to . . ." Ernie turned around and stopped dead. His face went white behind his mask.

Mark's regulator dangled loose in front of him. He slipped out of his turtle pack and handed it to Ernie, who took it in a slow, dazed motion.

"But you've got to know, Ernie," her voice went on, "because you're going to see . . ."

"Don't! Don't tell me nothin'! I don't wanna know nothin'!" He shook his head, as if she could see his emphatic gesture. He stared wide-eyed at Mark.

Mark lifted off his mask and handed it to Ernie.

Ernie saw his glowing green eyes for the first time—green even at that depth, almost luminescent. "Don't say any more." His eyes never left Mark. "He's a terrific guy . . . and . . . whatever he's had done to him is . . . is . . . okay with me. He's . . ."

His voice trailed off as he watched Mark. Mark's face and head were now completely exposed. His hair waved free in the water. No air bubbles were emitted from his nose or mouth. He slipped off the platform into the gray ocean. Once in the open water, he stripped off his wet suit, leaving him clad only in his tight swim trunks. He put the wet suit back on the platform at Ernie's feet. Then he began swimming back and forth, undulating smoothly, and went through a series of acrobatic spins, twists, somersaults—all manner of playful maneuvers.

He stopped, waved quickly to Ernie, flipped upside down, and shot downward out of sight.

"He's," Ernie's voice was a near-whisper as he watched Mark disappear into the depths, "he's my . . . friend . . ." His mitted hands clutched Mark's diving gear like talons.

At the shipboard console, Elizabeth, seeing by her gauges that Mark was now descending alone, sensed Ernie's profound confusion. ". . . It's okay, Ernie, he'll be okay. His respiratory system is—different from ours. I'll explain when you're topside. Try to relax, Ernie, or you'll use too much air. We're bringing you up now. Just take it easy. Try to calm yourself . . ."

Her eyes were on the digital depth gauge. Mark's body was a slowly moving dot on the scope. The gauge registered wildly: 2,000, 3,000, 4,000. Sonar pinging began. "Decompression is ready and waiting for you. We'll have plenty of time to talk . . ."

The gauges continued to reel off the depths: 10,000,

15,000, 20,000. She sensed added tension behind her. The two aides had heard her side of the conversation, and they could see the numbers. She wondered if anybody could really believe what was happening.

But more than that she wondered whether it would all work, and whether it would all be worth it.

For a time, Mark continued his playful maneuvers as he wound his way downward. He zig-zagged among schools of fish and reached out to touch a glowing squid that flashed by. He grabbed a hunk of floating kelp and swallowed it.

He veered over to be closer to the steep canyon walls, and wove his way among some pinnacles of rock.

He stopped briefly and circled, checking his surroundings. He moved horizontally for several yards, then darted down through a gully of rocks covered with odd growths and living protuberances that humans seldom see.

Finally he neared the ocean floor. He swam eel-like above it, gazing at the terrain, until he saw the spot he was looking for, and settled down on his feet.

He looked around, studying the environment. He had no way of knowing how deep he was in feet—though he knew exactly how deep he was by his own senses and reckoning. He had no way of knowing that high above him, the gauge before Elizabeth's eyes held steady at 35,021 feet, and that the silver dot on the green scope, which represented him, had stopped. And he had no way of hearing what Elizabeth was announcing into her microphone: "He's on the bottom, Ernie, and he's okay."

Nor could he have imagined Ernie's stunned face

at hearing that announcement, and how his voice sounded when he replied to Elizabeth: "Thirty-five thousand feet . . . seven miles . . . My God . . ."

Mark stood looking around, his green eyes glistening in the darkness. He looked up and down the canyou walls that surrounded him. He heard strange underwater sounds—clicks and snaps and eerie, high-pitched whistles.

Mark knew he was not as far down as he could go—not yet. He swam over to the side of the cliff, examined it with his eyes and hands, then pressed the side of his head against the rock wall. The sounds were louder there, the odd, repeated cadences of the whistles. They were distant whale sounds, communications. But there was something else too, something slight, something that to Mark was as strange as whale sounds were familiar.

He turned around, peering in all directions. He probed along the edge of the cliff until he found his passageway. Then he moved off down the cliff into the deeper gloom.

As he descended along the face of the cliff, he kept his eyes trained on the rock. But there were no signs of recently inflicted scratches or gouges through the vegetation, no broken rocks or any other kind of trail that might be left by a damaged submarine falling through this chasm to its doom. Nothing was disturbed.

Back and forth he glided over the cliff face, studying the rock and growth. From time to time he cocked his head to listen to the unique underwater noises he detected: He seemed not so much distracted by them as simply aware, as a motorist becomes attuned to the slight variations of pulse and hum of his engine.

He moved across the chasm to probe the opposite wall. Quickly he traversed it several hundred yards back and forth, descending several yards with each pass.

At last he approached the true bottom, the deepest part of the trench. He swam over it, gazing down. Back and forth and in slow circles he patrolled, like a hungry hawk searching for prey. Nothing on the bottom caught his attention particularly; nothing seemed to startle him. He moved in and out of the lowest crevasses, glided over and around the deepest crags, as if all were familiar terrain.

It was not that nothing moved in his view. There was life of wide variety in that pit. The animals were small, tiny. There were minute, transparent shrimp and eels and spiny bugs, clans of feathery plant-like fish, families of spidery, sightless crabs. They were so small and blended in so with the flora and rock that ordinary human eyes might not detect them.

To Mark, they were highly visible, and their presence, drifting or crawling unagitatedly, indicated that all was in order.

He was sliding along the bottom, no more than a foot above it, when he stopped. He hung motionless in the water. Then slowly he rolled over so that he was facing up. He cocked his head. Then he froze, as still as a chameleon on a tree limb.

There was a slight and unusual sound in the water. A sound Mark had been vaguely aware of before he descended past the face of the cliff. But it had been far distant. He had noticed it, kept tabs on it. Now it was closer, more distinct.

It was approaching him. He waited.

First it was a dull throbbing sound. Then that sound

was accompanied by a high-pitched whine. These were not animal sounds. There was a metallic edge to them. Soon they were identifiable. The throbbing was the pulse of propellers; the whine was an engine, probably electric.

For several minutes Mark had not moved a muscle, not even to breathe.

At once, all the tiny animals suddenly scattered; Mark knew the source of the sounds was near.

And then he saw it. First there was a needle of light penetrating the ocean above him. Then he discerned a bulbous nose. It glided evenly through the water some yards above him and to the side. As it passed he saw it all.

A black submarine of four round sections like bathyspheres, with small portholes gleaming from the sides. Atop the first sphere was a conical conning tower. The sub was pushed along by two slowly spinning propellers.

This was not the sub he was looking for. Nor was it like anything he had ever seen before. As it passed and began moving slowly away from him, he had to make a rapid determination of whether the sub related to his mission or not.

If it did not, to follow it would waste valuable time. Mark was aware of the vulnerability of the ship high overhead on the surface of the Pacific. Anything restricted to the surface was more susceptible to climatory changes than were water-breathing denizens of the deep like him. And on the trip out to this area aboard the ship, he had sensed clearly that although they called it an oceangoing vessel, it was not truly a creature of the sea. It was only the best creation land dwellers could devise to allow them brief excursions out onto the water but above it, where they could breathe their air while afloat on his world. But if a sudden typhoon sprang up—which Mark knew was a possibility in these waters—the people would have to flee with their complicated raft. When such a storm had passed, they might return with their ship or they might not—he was unsure of their commitment to this mission, so little did he understand of their natures and will. Nor was he sure the ship could safely escape the surface winds before which it was so defenseless.

But if this strange sub somehow did relate to his mission, he could not afford to let it vanish.

All this was reviewed and reconciled in a twinkling of synapses in his brain.

He darted after the sub, closing on it quickly. Then he cruised behind it and a bit below, keeping out of the spiraling wake left by the twin propellers.

Elizabeth rubbed her eyes. She had been staring at the white dot on the green scope for a long time. She flexed her shoulders to loosen the tension from sitting in one position for too long. She figured Ernie must be uncomfortable too, probably feeling the chill by now, as he was still being slowly reeled in.

When she looked back at the scope, she was startled. She peered at it for an instant. Then she leaned toward the mike. "Ernie, there's something else down there . . ."

A new white dot had appeared on the scope, moving slowly toward the dot that represented Mark.

"There's something else on the scope."

"What? What do you see?"

She was briefly relieved to hear Ernie's firm reply.

"Something else down there with Mark, moving toward him."

"Whale?"

"No. Too deep. And its motion is too regular. It's moving forward in a straight line. And it must be metallic, electronic, since I'm picking it up."

"Well, what . . ."

"It's getting closer . . . practically on top of him now . . . It's passing him . . . Moving away . . ."

She took a deep breath and put a hand on her forehead. "You'll be up in a minute, Ernie. I'll keep you posted in decompression."

"Roger."

"Mark is moving now."

"What?"

"Mark's signal is moving. He's following the thing . . ."

Mark trailed the sub easily, never taking his eyes off it. It turned to the right around a ledge of rock, then cruised between two towering pinnacles.

Suddenly, directly ahead of the sub but still a hundred yards away, a bright amber light appeared. As the sub continued forward, another light came on, then a third. They formed a triangle. The sub was aimed for the center of it.

Sonar pinging reached Mark's ears, and the volume increased as the sub approached the midpoint among the lights.

Then to either side of the sub, two rows of lights flashed on sequentially, like approach lights to an airport. The sub maintained a course between them. Two more powerful beams shot forward from the nose of the sub. They illuminated a huge steel door embedded in a mountain wall. The three amber lights of the triangle rimmed the door.

The sub slowed. Mark slowed equally. The engine noise and throbbing of the propellers diminished. The sonar pinging, however, increased in volume.

The sub gradually adjusted its depth, dropping a few feet to be in line with the mammoth gate.

Then there was a loud hum. The gate began to lift. The interior of a giant cave beyond the gate was bathed in light—as bright as the inside of the Undersea Center.

The sub edged toward the open gate. Mark looked quickly around, turned frantically in brief indecision. Then he straightened, fixed his eyes on the retreating sub, and followed.

The sub inched through the door in the mountainside toward the interior dock. As soon as its props were clear, the gate began to lower. Mark dove for the narrowing slice of light.

He felt the closing door just graze his heels as he slid through. He stopped, submerged just under the surface. The lights blinded him momentarily. But he heard no sounds from the sub. The engines and propellers had stopped.

Elizabeth had watched silently, biting her lip, for several minutes as Mark's dot had followed the other. She had watched them turn together, watched them wind around the unseen canyons on the ocean floor.

Then suddenly the sonar pinging stopped, the tiny silver dots disappeared. The scopes were silent and blank. Her hands leaped for the dials and controls, she spun them feverishly. But there was nothing.

She sank back into her chair. "He's gone," she said softly.

Sunlight filtered through from the nearing surface, a halo above Ernie's rising platform.

"He's gone," he heard her whisper.

Ernie stared down into the gloom through which Mark had disappeared from him, and now from them all.

## chapter 6

When Mark's eyes adjusted to the bright lights, he could see that the sub had surfaced. They were in a narrow concrete waterway, just wide enough to give the sub a cozy berth. A concrete walkway surrounded them. Stark concrete walls curved into a high, arched concrete ceiling where dozens of bright lights were embedded.

Interspersed with the light, and at various spots on the walls, were camera lenses, like small eyes.

The hoisting and loading equipment and other electronic machinery of the dock was confined to an area in front of the sub. Otherwise, the entire dock was bare, pristine, sterile-white.

Most surprising of all was the absence of any people or movement in the dock. Mark had stayed partly submerged, expecting at any moment to see the flood of attendants and dock workers that he was used to seeing attend a mooring at the Center. But no one came.

He surfaced and moved toward the silent sub.

Just then the hatch in the side of the conning tower opened and heads appeared.

Mark ducked under the water and moved quickly to the side of the channel, sliding under the lip of the walkway. It was always his instinct to hide cautiously until he was able to analyze a new situation—that was what kept him alive in his undersea environment, where beings strange to one another cannot sit down and discuss their attitudes and intentions.

Three men and one woman stepped out of the hatch onto the ramp and proceeded to the walkway. They stopped in a cluster and looked around, as if this place was new to them also.

They were not dressed like Navy or even like civilian ship personnel. Two of the men were wearing dark suits and ties, one had a blue sports jacket on over an open-necked flowered shirt. The woman was wearing a powder-blue jumpsuit and a frilly white blouse.

They stood uncomfortably together, looking this way and that as if expecting someone. They spoke English, but the accents varied.

"Beautiful day," the woman said, with a wry smile, looking around at the enclosure. Her intonations were French.

The others laughed nervously.

"Clean enough to do surgery in here." Nasal American. "Makes me miss the old lab."

"Is clean like Moscow subway." Russian inflections.

"It certainly doesn't remind me of anything, I must say." Clipped British. "Wonder if we should be off somewhere, or just stand here, or . . ."

"Welcome." A clear, amplified voice came from somewhere. Their heads spun around, looking for the source, not finding it. "We are pleased to see that you are all well and in good spirits. As per your briefing instructions, you will first change into appropriate attire for your work here. Please proceed to the changing rooms, as indicated by the sign . . ."

A light flashed on above them on the wall. It spelled out CHANGING ROOMS, followed by an arrow indicating a corridor just then revealed as a door slid open in the concrete.

"Then follow corridor 14 to your reception desk. We are happy to have you with us. We are sure your eminent qualifications as scientists will serve us all well in our endeavors within the habitat."

The scientists looked at each other, then turned and headed through the door and off down the corridor.

Mark quickly emerged from the water, swung himself onto the walkway, and quietly followed.

Up the corridor, the three men stopped, looked up and down at a door marked CHANGING—M, and went in. The woman went through the next door marked CHANGING—F.

Mark stepped back around a bend and waited.

Soon the scientists emerged dressed alike in two-piece white clean-room suits and white slipper-shoes. They stood and looked at each other and themselves, chuckling occasionally.

"I think I look like a Grand Prix driver," the woman said.

"Nice material," said the Russian, fingering his sleeve, "expensive."

"Well, we look official now," said the American. "Sure gonna miss the World Series."

They all laughed, except for the British scientist, who examined his garb soberly. "At least it's a better life than missiles."

They all nodded, looked around, saw the lighted sign that indicated corridor 14, and headed off down it.

Mark started to enter the corridor behind them, then stepped back. For some distance ahead, there was no place to conceal himself. Corridor 14 was an absolutely straight concrete tunnel—white with high curving walls like the dock—with indirect overhead lighting.

Mark listened to the soft footsteps of the scientists in the corridor. He also heard other soft sounds, mechanical ones. He could identify the rhythmic thrust of hydraulic pumps coming from somewhere within the walls.

At the distant end of the corridor, in an alcove off to the side, was a wide desk behind which sat three young women dressed like the approaching scientists. One woman was black, with a neat Afro. One was white, with blond hair pulled into a bun at the back of her head. The third was Oriental, with almond eyes and black hair cropped short around the ears.

The scientists came to the end of the corridor, turned, and uneasily confronted the three women.

The black woman smiled and handed out white cards to each of them. "Good morning. I see your clothes fit you well. Would you register, please? Just fill out the cards, answering each of the questions. Leave no blanks, please."

The scientists nodded and took the cards and said thank you. The cards asked for names and addresses, places of birth, current nationality, names of parents, age and sex, and whom to notify in case of emergency.

The woman handed them ball-point pens, and they bent over the desk to fill out the cards.

The British scientist did not immediately begin to write. He studied his card.

The second woman opened a drawer and took out a metal box and opened it. It was full of flexible metal wristbands in various solid hues. "And would you like to put on your color-coded identification bracelets, please? You'll find them very helpful here."

The three women behind the desk were wearing such bracelets.

The British scientist tapped his card with the pen and looked at the women. "Where is Mr. Schubert? We were supposed to meet him straight away."

"Yes, of course," said the black woman, smiling. "He's rather busy this morning, but he'll see you right after orientation."

The Frenchwoman accepted a bracelet for herself, then took another from the box and handed it to the Russian.

The Russian held his up in front of him and smiled at it. "Is like my very own Mickey Mouse."

They and the American laughed lightly. Then they snapped on their bracelets, and their laughter abruptly ceased.

The black woman put a bracelet on the desk beside the British scientist's card. He looked at it but did not pick it up. "Mr. Schubert said we would all be working together in the high-energy lab," he said stiffly.

"Why don't you register and slip on your bracelet," the black woman cooed, smiling more warmly. "I'm sure everything will be in order."

The other three scientists were completely still. The Britisher frowned and looked dourly around, noticing a small camera lens high on the wall, aimed at them. "Listen, before signing anything, I'd like to verify that the facilities are as advertised, and that no military applications are permitted."

"Here," said the Oriental woman in delicate tones, picking up the bracelet, "let me put it on for you."

The Britisher leaned forward, clomping his knuckles down on the desk. "See here, we all insist that . . ."

The woman snapped the bracelet on his wrist. He straightened up. His face no longer showed concern, but was calm and placid. He relaxed.

"Now then," the black woman pushed the card in front of him. "Would you fill in the card, please?"

He dutifully filled in the card. The others stood watching him.

"Thank you." The woman took the card along with the others and slid them into a card-file box. "Now," she rose and beckoned, "would you all follow me, please? Right this way." She stepped off toward a side corridor, beckoning continually. The four scientists docilely followed.

When the four had earlier left the changing rooms and headed down corridor 14, Mark had waited a moment, then ducked into the men's changing room. When they were at the desk, he had come out and edged down the corridor, listening to their confusing conversations, timing his entrance for when they had cleared the area.

Now, dressed like them in a white clean-room suit, he came up to the desk.

"Good morning, sir," said the woman with blond hair. "Let's see," she checked a yellow sheet in front of her on the desk, "we were expecting four . . ."

The Oriental woman leaned over to scan the sheet with her. "Yes, but . . ."

"But they could have meant five." The first woman looked up at Mark and smiled. "Mathematicians have their own ways with numbers, do they not?"

"Yes."

She reached into the box. "Would you like to put on your color-coded identification bracelet?"

"What is that?"

"Here," she took out a red one and reached for his wrist, "let me do it." She slipped it around his wrist and snapped it shut. "There. Now, so that we may get on with the program, would you enter and sign in, please?" She slid a card toward him.

Mark held his wrist up and looked at the bracelet, then looked back at the woman. She smiled, but he did not smile back. He put his other hand over his wrist as he looked at her. His knuckles turned white, as if under tension. When his hand came away it was holding the disconnected bracelet. He handed it to her. "I do not need a color-coded identification bracelet."

The faces of the two women remaining at the desk suddenly lost their smiles and went blank.

The mouth of the Oriental woman moved mechanically, her voice calm, but without the prior lilt. "We all must wear our bracelets here. It is for our comfort and well-being. I suggest that you reconsider. It is in your interest to comply with our—"

"Aha!"

A door opened above and behind the desk, under a large pulsing red light and atop a ramp that emerged from the wall. Through the door stepped a big, bald, round-faced smiling man in a rumpled brown suit. "Here's yet another!" He waddled down the ramp toward Mark, grinning and extending his hand. "Aha. Welcome, young man." He took Mark's hand and squeezed it slightly. "It's a pleasure to meet you. I am Mr. Schubert, of course." He slid his hand up to

Mark's shoulder and steered him around the desk.

They started up the ramp, Schubert a half-step behind. "You've given us a nice surprise, young man. We expected four new members for our society, and we got five. Good investment, don't you think? Put your efforts into a goal of four, and receive a surprise bonus of twenty-five percent. I would say that's a splendid return. Right through here, young man."

He shoved Mark gently through the door, then stepped through it himself. The door closed behind them. They proceeded down a corridor. Schubert glanced up at the row of red lights on the wall, and narrowed his eyes briefly as he saw that they continued to flash.

"Tell me, my fine fellow, how did you manage to get here?"

"I swam."

"Swam!" He laughed a deep, rumbling laugh. "Aha! That's a good one! Yes indeed. You must be an American. Such a sense of humor. Good for the soul. Keeps the juices flowing. And I suppose the fish told you how to reach our door?"

"I do not know the language of fish. The inner current took me to the deep sound channel and I listened to the whales talk . . ."

"The whales! My, my, my. Heh-heh." He tapped Mark lightly on the back. "Well, it's a fact that they do, in their way, but—"

"I felt the presence of your submarine far off and waited for it. Then I followed it."

"Hmmm." His eyes wrinkled cheerfully. "You do a lot of that, do you? Wait for a submarine as you might a bus? And follow the submarine through pitch-black wilderness at the bottom of uncharted oceans seven miles beneath the surface? Why, that's marvelous! Stupendous! Extraordinary! My friend, you're a very clever fellow. A tale I must remember to relate to Mark Twain, should I ever run across the geezer in the land beyond."

His belly shivered with a deep chuckle. He took Mark's arm lightly and they stopped. He looked into Mark's green eyes, and narrowed his own. "By the way, I apologize for that little, um, problem with the identification bracelet. I understand completely. Personally, I can't abide them either." He reached into his jacket pocket. "But most people in these environs find they come in handy. Give you a feeling of well-being and security. So here," he took out a bracelet, "take mine."

Deftly he seized Mark's hand and slipped the bracelet on his wrist. Then he turned Mark forward again and they resumed their stroll.

His voice now took on a less jovial tone, became more businesslike. The red lights along the corridor continued to flash. "Now then, suppose you tell me who you are and what's your purpose in being here."

"I am . . . Mark Harris."

"Aha. Mark Harris. Doesn't ring a bell. So be it. And the rest?"

Mark turned to look at him. He lifted his arm. The bracelet dangled from his fingers. "I do not need this . . . for well-being."

"I see." Schubert gingerly took the bracelet from Mark's fingers and put it back in his pocket. "Impressive bit of sleight-of-hand, to be literal about it." He pinched his lips together and studied Mark's eyes. The flashing red lights reflected off his bald head as if the pate itself were pulsing. "I see. You're quite an unusual fellow, Mark Harris. May I call you Mark? Quite uncommon indeed. We'll have to learn more about you, much more. But there's a time and place for everything. I can see that your, um, aquatic adventures have left you rather tired. Altogether natural. Quite a little dip in the ocean, I must say. Well then, let's move along. You'll get some rest now. And later on I'll show you what some peaceful scientists have created at the bottom of the sea."

They walked through corridors under blinking red lights, making a turn here and there. Mark was conscious of the heavy man's labored breathing; Schubert was just as conscious of Mark's.

"From time to time," Schubert said, his voice softer, "we all need a little reminder that we still have a few 'I's' to dot and 'T's' to cross before we get the results of a rather interesting experiment we're working on here. But it's all going to click into place shortly, with the help of a few mathematical types—the very ones who came on the sub," he laughed, "the sub you accompanied."

Mark looked at him, his face showing nothing.

"Right over here then," he gestured toward a door. "You'll get some rest. And when you wake, refreshed and relaxed—aha! I'll have some interesting things to show and discuss with you!"

Elizabeth, still at her console, where the sonar scope was silent and the green screen blank, was talking on a red phone. Ernie, in clean work blues, sat on a folding canvas chair nearby.

". . . We brought up the diver, Ernie Davis. He's

fine, no effects at all. Except of course he's as concerned as we all are. And Commander Johnson has ordered an S & R unit."

"What the devil good is a search unit going to do!" came Admiral Pierce's exasperated, angry voice over the line. "The only thing that could go down there is the same *Sea Quest* your man was after!"

Elizabeth heard his hoarse breathing over the phone. "Well, sir, we . . ."

"With all the precautions we've taken, all the instructions we've given, all the work and worry and negotiations—I don't see how you could lose him!"

"We've been trying to—"

"We had a deal, Dr. Merrill!"

"I'm well aware of that, sir." Her face flashed anger, she struggled to keep her voice calm. "The deal was that he would find the *Sea Quest* in exchange for his freedom. Well, he—"

"And he took off!"

"No sir!" Rage welled up in her. She gripped the receiver tightly and glared at the console. "I'm sure that's not it. He wouldn't do that. He *didn't* do that."

"Well, what other explanation . . ."

"He just fell off the scope, Admiral."

"Fell off the scope!"

"Yes, sir."

"Well then check the scope! Those things aren't perfect."

"We did, sir. And we have backup equipment."

"You gave him the transponder?"

"Of course. We had the signal."

"Well maybe your fish digested the darn thing!"

"Admiral! I resent your referring to Mark Harris as my—"

"Sorry. Sorry. Forgive me. I know what you must be going through. Just try to understand, I'm sitting in here like a dumb landlubber, staring out my window, helpless to do anything, with so much of my work riding on this mission—so much of yours too. I should have gone out there with you."

"I don't think it would have helped, sir. Nothing would have changed. Preparations were perfect. All systems were functioning optimally. He reached the bottom in good shape. Then he just disappeared."

There was a silence on the line.

Ernie leaned forward and whispered, "Does the admiral know that—know what Mark . . ."

Elizabeth nodded.

"Well listen, Dr. Merrill," came his voice finally, "our job has become a good deal more complicated, to put it simply. First we were supposed to find the *Sea Quest*. Now we've got to find the one who was supposed to find the *Sea Quest*." He paused. "I'm keeping a line open for any news. I want to be informed of *anything*, any development, large or small, positive or negative."

"Yes sir."

"Find him."

"Have a drink, Ainsley. The admiral shoved a glass and a bottle of Guatemalan rum across the desk at the lieutenant.

"No thank you, sir." Ainsley sat stiffly in the armchair and held up his palm.

"Have one, Ainsley," he growled. Then he smiled wryly. "You don't approve."

"Oh, no sir, it's not that. I have nothing against a little drink now and then."

"But you don't approve of *me* having a little drink, right now, under these circumstances."

"Oh, no sir," he shook his head vigorously, "it's not that. Whatever you do is your, is your . . ."

"Business, Ainsley. My business. I am very much on duty, Ainsley. And I am thinking. I am thinking hard. Have a drink. That's an order."

"Yes sir. Fine." He took the bottle and poured a small amount into the glass. "Just one."

"No such thing." The admiral raised his glass for a toast, and Ainsley lifted his. The admiral tilted his head back and threw it down. Ainsley sipped a bit and put his glass on the desk.

"No, no, Lieutenant. The first one goes down neat and quick, all at once. Gets your thought processes moving. You gotta break your brain outta the rut first with a hard shove from the rum. Then you can coast. Sip the second one. Come on, toss her down."

"Yes sir." Ainsley picked up the glass, closed his eyes, and drank it down. He blinked and wiped his mouth with his fingers.

"There." The admiral leaned back and smiled. "Pour another, and let's talk."

Ainsley poured another.

"Now. What's on your mind, Lieutenant?"

"Sir?" Ainsley coughed lightly.

"Speak out. What do you think about all this, man to man?"

"About all what, sir?"

"Me, Dr. Merrill, Mark Harris, the mission—everything."

"Oh. I haven't thought much about it."

"Cowpies, Ainsley. You haven't been thinking about

much else *but* lately. Same as me. You think I've made a mistake. Or several."

"No sir."

"Look, Ainsley," he leaned across the desk, "I'd rather you just didn't answer rather than lie to me. This is just between us. You think, number one, I shouldn't have trusted Dr. Merrill so completely. Hunh?"

"Well," he said softly, looking at the floor, "it's just that she's a scientist, not really a Navy officer, and . . ."

"It's just that she's a woman, right? You don't care beans whether she's a scientist or a Marine. It bothers you that I leave a woman with so much responsibility."

Ainsley opened his mouth.

"Don't speak."

He closed it.

"I know it's the truth. She ain't just another pretty face, buddy. Not *just* another pretty face. She is absolutely brilliant. Did you know that? And here's another newsflash for you: she is one very tough Navy man. How's that grab you? Tough as the toughest old sea captain you'll ever meet. She knows what she's doing and she knows how to do it and she'll fight for being allowed to do her job. Just like I will. Will you fight to be allowed to do your job, Ainsley?"

Ainsley opened his mouth silently.

"Talk."

"Yes sir. My answer is yes, I will, sir."

"More cowpies, my boy. You're scared to death to take a step on your own. Let me tell you something about command. You'd like to have your own command someday. Well, command is not a set of theories that you go around asking other people for answers about. It is not a discussion group. It is not therapy. It is not hemming and hawing and seeing all sides and taking none. It is decisions. A command is like a computer—a series of firm yesses and nos. Yes, you go; no, you stop. You have a mission, you have your matériel, you have your personnel. Will it work? Yes, you go; no, you don't. And that's it. There's no time for wondering about all the ways a mission might fail, once you're moving, or all the ways it might succeed, once you've killed it. You pick a yes or you pick a no. If you're good, you pick 'em right most of the time. That's all there is to it."

Ainsley sipped his drink and nodded thoughtfully. "That's really beautifully put, sir."

"Ah, me." The admiral sighed and swiveled back and forth and stared at the ceiling. "And another thing that's rather quaint about what's on your mind, son. You think Mark Harris is some kind of fraud."

"Fraud, sir?"

"You don't really believe all this stuff about what he can do. Why not?"

"Sir, I'm in no position to doubt . . ."

The admiral banged his fist on the desk, causing some papers and the lieutenant to jump. "Say it straight out!"

"It's just that no man can breathe under water!" he blurted. "Sir."

"Good, good. Now we're getting someplace." The admiral smiled. "Now tell me, how do you think he pulls this stunt off?"

"I don't know."

"You don't know." The admiral chuckled. "Now, imagine yourself in command here. You find some jerko washed up on the beach. You get him revived and cleaned up. You put him through some tests. You *see* those tests yourself, just as you and I have. You see him stay under water for hours, even sleep under water. You see him dive to thirty thousand feet in the pressure tank. You see him race a dolphin and win. You see him dig a torpedo out of the mud and bring it up faster than a CURV. You witness all this. You can doubt it all you want. Try to figure it out. You figure the jerko's got an angle, and one day you'll put your finger on his tricks. Right?"

"Yes sir."

"Sure. Then you lose the *Sea Quest* down in the Mariana. You got nothing that can go down there after it. Except maybe Jerko. Your Houdini there. Maybe he can work his magic one more time and find the *Sea Quest.*" The admiral poured two more glasses of rum. "You haven't got time to figure him out. You got time for a yes or a no. And it's up to you, Commander Ainsley. What do you say?"

"I don't know."

"Wanna be a lieutenant for the rest of your life, and a go-fer for the admiral?"

"No sir. I mean . . ."

"Do you dive the jerko, yes or no?"

"Yes."

"Good. Yes is right. You dive him. But that's the easy part, right?"

"Easy?"

"Yes or no is easy, comparatively. Now comes the harder part. You lose Jerko. The whole shebang falls apart. What do you do now?"

"I don't know, sir."

"You think, Lieutenant Ainsley. You think hard. Now's the time you try to figure it all out. You think like you never thought before. You wring your brain. You got to come up with something. Isn't that right?"

"Yes sir."

"And here's the hardest part of all: you come up blank. You sit here in this chair, commanding this important mission, you are faced with total failure, and you can't think of anything to do. Ain't that a fix, Lieutenant Ainsley?"

"Yes sir. It surely is, sir."

"And what're you gonna do about it?"

"Me, sir?"

"You. I'll tell you what you're gonna do. You're gonna put all your doubts and second-guesses aside. You're gonna support your admiral inside and out, heart and soul. You're gonna think about Dr. Merrill out on that ship and Mark Harris seven miles underneath it, and you're gonna hope with all you got that somehow they can put this thing back together and get out of it. You know why?"

"Unh, well . . ."

"'Cause I put em there, Ainsley."

Elizabeth finally allowed herself to be relieved at the console, agreeing that so long as the detectors were picking up nothing, a qualified technician might just as well stare at the monitors for a while.

She was supposed to rest, but instead she took Ernie Davis to the debriefing room. She poured them both some coffee and sat across the table from him.

The eyes of both were red-rimmed with weariness. For a moment they both stared at the black porthole. There were no stars, no moon, nothing visible out in the night. The bridge reported clouds, maybe some rain, but no storm expected.

"Okay, Ernie," she said finally, "give it back to me, piece by piece."

"Gee, Doctor," he slowly turned his coffee mug in his hands and stared at it, "I don't know what I can add to what you already know. We went down easy, you know, to two hundred. I'll admit I was curious about the guy. I liked him, but there was something different about him, you know? But it wasn't worrying me none. He seemed to know what he was doing. I had my mind on the dive.

"Then we got down there to two hundred, and I was testing my line, and talking to you. Then I seen him take off his gear. Like, I gotta admit, I was really stunned. I don't even remember what he took off first and second and like that. I was just dumfounded, you might say."

"How was he acting? What was his mood?"

"Well, he's like, you never could tell what his mood was. He didn't smile or nothin'. Except for what he was doing, which shocked me down there, he seemed to be just like before—serious, quick, efficient. He just took off his stuff and handed it to me and stepped off the platform."

"And then?"

"It was strange. Everything was, you might say. But it was strange how he acted in the open water. He started doing all sorts of gymnastics and stuff, you know, spinning around, head over heels, bobbing and weaving, that kind of stuff."

"Right next to the platform."

"Yes, in fact. Almost like he was putting on a show for me."

"Did it seem like he was reflecting some kind of mood then?"

"Yes it did. It did. Again, he didn't smile. But I would say, from the way he was behaving, he was happy. That's how I would describe it. Happy as a kid just let out of school, or a guy just let out of jail. But then suddenly he stopped all that, waved to me, and took off straight down."

"Now Ernie, this may be a hard thing to answer, because I'm asking you for a guess. But did you have any feeling at all that he might have been so happy swimming freely out there that he would just abandon the mission and go away?"

Ernie thought for a moment. "Just before he went out of sight, he stopped one more time to give me the thumbs-up. To my way of thinking, as a diver, that means just one thing: you're gonna go ahead and do your job."

She nodded slowly, took a sip of coffee, and leaned across the table. "Now, Ernie. Anything you want to ask me? About Mark Harris or the mission?"

"No, ma'am, if you don't mind. I got an inkling, from your conversations and stuff. Just now I'd rather know only what I gotta know to be helpful. I'll do anything you want. I'm ready to dive, go down on a recovery—whatever."

"Thanks, Ernie." She smiled and tapped his arm. "We've really got a good team."

"Yeah. Except that the best part of it's wandering around down there on the bottom of the ocean, running into who knows what kinda trouble."

"You think he's down there then, still functioning?"

"Just a feeling. But you know as well as I do, when you dive a lot, and get used to working deep, you get to trust your feelings. I got a feeling Mark Harris is down there somewhere tryin' to do his job." He paused. "Or maybe not."

"That about sums it up, Ernie, I guess."

## chapter 7

It was not rest Mark needed, but water. The room into which he was guided and left alone contained a double bunk, a dresser, a mirror, a closet, and a shower.

As soon as Schubert had shut the door and left, Mark pulled off his clean-room suit and stepped into the shower. He turned the cold water on full and tipped his face to the nozzle, leaning virtually against it, directing the spray into his mouth.

He stayed that way for approximately as long as one would be expected to take a nap.

He was still not sure how or even if this undersea complex related to his assigned mission of locating the *Sea Quest*. But until the submarine appeared on the scene, he had found nothing unusual in the trench. And Mr. Schubert's operation was in the general area of his search. If the *Sea Quest* lay someplace near where the Navy thought it did, it was likely that Mr. Schubert would know something about it. If not likely, at least possible.

But it was Mark's instinct to approach any new situtation cautiously, watching and listening before revealing his own intentions. It had been the same at the Undersea Center with Dr. Merrill.

Here he would not yet reveal his mission, because what Mr. Schubert was all about was still a mystery to him.

Finally he turned off the shower—it wasn't enough, but it would do for a while. He dried himself and lay down on the bunk, waiting for the knock on the door that would summon him to the promised revelations by Mr. Schubert.

"Come in, come in," Schubert beckoned to the French woman scientist, "let's have it."

She entered his office, followed by a lean, gray-haired man with a badge pinned to his chest that said SUPERVISOR. She put a sheaf of papers on the desk in front of Schubert.

He bent quickly over the papers, which were scientific readouts, and examined them closely, flipping them over one after another.

The woman and the supervisor stood silently.

"Hmm, grmmp, fsss," came the mumblings from his mouth. His lips moved incessantly as he scanned the papers, tracing his index finger under certain lines, tapping it on certain others.

At last he leaned back and scowled. "Garbage. Incorrect, imprecise, out of tune. I could have got better stuff from an M.I.T. freshman. It doesn't add up. It doesn't jibe. It wouldn't work. If I used these numbers here, the computers would spit them right back out at me, laughing as they did."

"The mathematicians are redoing the computations," the woman said in a monotone.

"Well, they better get cracking or we're going to miss the bus. Get these chicken tracks out of my sight."

She quickly scooped up the papers and backed away from the desk.

"Go."

She left.

"Now then, George." He nodded to the supervisor, who stepped up to the desk. "I need that other report, about our unexpected visitor. I want to know exactly what I have here. Where does that stand?"

"It is underway."

"Underway, underway. I wish I had a penny for everything around here that was underway but unfinished. Where does it stand?"

"So far we have his name, and—"

"He told me his name, for heaven's sake, hours ago! What else have you got?"

"There is not much to report, as yet. The investigators are having difficulty assigning and assessing certain components and characteristics. Our sensors seem confused by his emanations. And others in the new group seem unfamiliar with him."

"Difficulty, confused, unfamiliar. That is not the stuff by which solutions are arrived at, George."

"Ordinarily, Mr. Schubert, we would have a chance to interview and observe a subject for whom you wished to compile a dossier. The whole procedure would be simplified if he were wearing the prescribed color-coded identification bracelet."

"Yes, yes, George. That's the first paragraph on page six of the operations manual. I don't need it quoted. I wrote it, as you may be aware. Well, we have no time for ordinary procedures. I will myself have to dope him out. Get on with your duties, George. Time's a-wasting."

George backed away from the desk.
"Go."

When the knock came on the door, Mark, in his clean-room suit, was standing before the mirror, examining his eyes and nose and mouth as if looking for symptoms of something. He started for the door when it opened. A pale man in a similar outfit stepped in.

"Would you follow me, please?"

They walked through some corridors and arrived at a broad steel door. The man held his palm under a small purple light beside the door, and it lifted. He motioned Mark through, then turned and walked back the way they had come.

Mark found himself in a vast cavern of labs and tanks and electronic equipment. Several scientists bustled around the equipment and tanks, taking readings from gauges, writing things on clipboards, pressing buttons, pulling levers, turning wheels.

Here and there, contrasting with the scurrying, white-clad people and the humming, sophisticated equipment, were ancient statues, mosaics, urns, coral-encrusted jugs, eroded marble faces, terra-cotta dolphins—recognizable to Mark as booty from the sea—all spotlighted dramatically from concealed beams.

In the large tanks swam several varieties of fishes and other sea animals.

"Ah, yes," Schubert came forward, smiling, "Mark Harris. I thought you might be interested in our laboratories. I daresay you've never seen anything like it, for nothing like it exists in the world. Our experiments here can, in fact, change the course of life on this planet."

He steered Mark over to a tank where several sea turtles swam lazily.

"What we are doing here, quite simply, is associating ourselves with the future of mankind. The future is not land, but water. Nearly three-fourths of our globe is covered with water, my boy. Land is not permanent. The continents are moving. The Americas, Africa—all are slipping and sliding one way or another. Not fast enough to make you lose your balance, mind you. It takes centuries. But they are moving. Some have even disappeared—but I won't get into all that now. It would only serve to confuse you. But the fact is, the oceans have more energy, more power, more nutriments, larger mammals, taller mountains—bigger and better everything—than those impermanent dry hunks of real estate upstairs. And those humans who invest all their chips in land are going to be rudely disappointed when the sea age comes."

Schubert elbowed Mark gently. "And the sea age is coming sooner than anybody thinks, my boy. Because we are creating it, right here. We have developed mankind's first home and society on the ocean floor. And not a bad job of it, do you think?" He gestured grandly. "We are quite comfortable, the air is clean, everybody has a job and three highly nutritional meals a day. Plus we are absorbed in the greatest of all challenges: We are creating and expanding our world here, so that when the time comes—and it's just around the corner—we shall be prepared to live forever, through future generations, protected from the elements, in the safety of the eternal sea. Interesting and exciting, wouldn't you say?"

Mark said nothing.

They moved along among the tanks, stopping to

look into each of them. "Before we came along," Schubert went on, "the idea of a sea-mountain habitat was just a bunch of chicken tracks on a piece of paper. It was all theory and sand castles in the deep. A few absentminded professors were interested in it —mainly because they made their livings pondering matters that nobody cared about. But nowhere among the mighty nations was the bottom of the oceans perceived with anything but ignorance and contempt. There was no money in it. You couldn't sell any Buicks or Cadillacs there, or fast-hamburgers. You couldn't set up bank branches, or movie studios, or World Trade Centers. You couldn't hold the World Series there, or the Super Bowl, or political conventions.

"In short, the ocean depths provided none of the opportunities for development of things that mankind's movers and shakers thought made the world go round. But we were not so shortsighted. We saw where the future would be. And we made it work. And I'll tell you the secret: make friends with the ocean. Good advice for you too, Mark—make friends with the ocean."

They moved over to the section of tables and electronic consoles and gadgets and burners and bubbling vials and tubes and coils and bottles and steaming trays and tanks of various compressed gasses. A small man with wispy blond hair and long, delicate fingers moved among the equipment, peering at things, making adjustments, tapping gauges.

"Here now," Schubert said, touching the man's shoulder, "Emil, tell us what you're up to."

Emil spoke in the same monotone Mark heard from everyone there except Schubert. "Our ultimate aim is to adapt ourselves to life in the ocean by creating *homo aquatis*—a water-breathing man. By associating and blending certain gasses and diffusing them through certain tissues in saline solution, we are approaching the time when we can accommodate the differentials between dissimilar partial pressures of oxygen and nitrogen, whose requirements of balance between man's cardiovascular system and the atmosphere have allowed him to breathe air but have not heretofore yielded to the requirements for man's similar breathing of water."

"Tut-tut, Emil, a bit complicated for our new man here. Not sure I follow the little egghead myself, Mark, although I know what he means. Tell me, Mark, do you believe it's possible to develop a water-breathing man?"

"When he learns to breathe water . . . he will be other . . . than a man."

"A most philosophical observation." Schubert studied him through narrowed eyes. "How very charming. Not terribly relevant, but how nice to hear someone express a thought around here."

Mark turned up the corners of his mouth, copying Schubert's smile.

"What he means, simply, is that through certain transplants and grafts, and thenceforth natural evolution, we shall soon have a man who can breathe water like a fish. Don't laugh. We're already well along. You may see such an adaptation in your lifetime."

Schubert paused, as if expecting Mark to chuckle. Seeing no flicker of amusement on the green-eyed face, he turned to a bank of shallow metal drawers and pulled one open. It contained a tray of black squares the size and consistency of bouillon cubes. "When it comes to ocean science, my good man, we're quantum jumps ahead of the rest of them. Even the Chinese—who, unbeknownst to you Americans, are significantly more advanced than the rest of the surface world in experimentation with the possibilities of water. Everything here in our habitat comes from the sea—power, air, light, food, everything."

He picked up one black square and held it out to Mark. "Taste it."

Mark studied it without touching it.

"Go ahead, it won't kill you. Trust me. Go on, have a bite."

Mark reached out his hand—the fingertips slightly brown in early dehydration—and took the square and popped it into his mouth. He chewed for a moment, then swallowed it. "Plankton," he said.

Schubert took a step backward, his eyes wide. "By golly, he's right. Plankton it is. Right on the nose. One of the most nutritious foods provided by the earth. My, my, my." He narrowed his eyes. "I figure you to be a marine biologist. Am I right? You heard about us from some loose-lipped colleague up in Santa Barbara or Wood's Hole and stowed away on our shuttle to see for yourself." He stood beaming with satisfaction.

"I am a citizen of . . . the ocean."

"Then we have a lot in common." He took a square himself and tossed it into his mouth and chewed vigorously. "I was a seagoing junkman for twenty years—Bali to Boston, Vladivostok to Venice, Santiago to Sydney—until I got smart. I had collected from the sea beds artifacts that would boggle the mind of any museum. You see examples throughout the habitat. But finally I got smart. Who wants to spend his life boggling the minds of dusty old museums? Nobody up there really appreciated these treasures from the sea.

I appreciated them so much I even wanted to be *part* of the sea, submerge myself and be independent of all that topside clutter we call civilization.

"But I needed money. So I made one final world-wide scavenge and sold it all—except for what few things I have here—to a bunch of wheezing old teary-eyed museum masters for more money than Midas. And I began my project. And now that I *am* smart, *and* rich, *and*, if I may so, imaginative and daring, I do what I want. And I am in the process of making the greatest contribution to mankind that has ever been contemplated. In time these figurines of Neptune and all the rest will symbolize the new society. Mine, of course."

Schubert wrinkled his pudgy face in a broad smile, put his arm around Mark's shoulders, and raised his other arm and moved it in a slow arc through the air. "All this, and everything and everybody in it, is mine. Not bad for an ordinary Aquarius, wouldn't you say?"

Inside a small, dimly lit viewing room before banks of screens, two men stared at the central monitor. One was George, the supervisor. The other wore a pocket badge that said TECHNICIAN—AB2.

In the semi-darkness they gazed dully at the animated images on the screen. They were looking at computer images of systems in Mark's body. His face and torso were shown on the screen, and flowing through them were dots of various colors.

"We are at plus-four," said the technician in his monotone. "Baseline studies are complete. TM is good. Wave formation is good. Neurons firing at ten to the minus-twenty."

George did not nod or acknowledge the statements

in any way. "Mr. Schubert requests priority scan of skin-structure anomalies."

"Please inform him that those remote readouts will proceed immediately. Would he prefer to see all this in the standard bound volumes?"

"No. He wants them hot. He has informed me that there is no time for standard procedures."

"Is he dissatisfied with my work?"

"No. He insists only on speed, at this point."

"Very well."

"You may be pleased to know that the mathematicians are lagging behind you once again."

"Thank you. That does enhance my sense of well-being."

Mark's tour continued into the mammal lab, where tiny overhead cameras continued to swivel to follow his movements. Here the tanks extended from floor to ceiling, with viewing ports at eye level. Mark and Schubert walked among the statuary and stepped up to a large tank. Mark leaned to peer through the port.

Two killer whales swam around and around, their white and black markings glistening under the lights. High-pitched whale sounds came from small amplifiers in the tank. Mark listened intently as he watched them circle.

"Freddie," Schubert motioned to a white-suited scientist nearby, "would you please tell Mr. Harris what you are doing with the orcas here?"

The scientist bowed. "Orcas—or killer whales as you probably know them—are not fish but are, like other whales, mammals. Unlike other whales, however, they have a reputation for dangerous behavior. They will attack dolphins and seals, and even human beings, under some conditions. Their savagery is generally exaggerated, however, and we have them here because they are intelligent and cooperative. Being mammal, this whale has a culture and a refined system of communication. It is their communication with which we occupy ourselves in this section. Would you step this way, please?"

They moved away from the tank to the opposite side of the room, where there was a steel desk surrounded by audio equipment and graphs. As the whale sounds came over small stereo speakers, an electronic stylus traced squiggly lines on a graph.

Above Mark, a small sensor protruded a couple of inches from the ceiling, and in it a small purple light began to pulse.

"Here," the scientist said, "we are recording what we call, for lack of a better term, the whales' voices. These recordings will go over to cryptoanalysis, where the patterns and inflections of their squeaks are studied and will, in time, be translated into words or sentences or paragraphs—whatever meter and length the whales use. Computer translation of their language is imminent. Mr. Schubert is interested in learning what they might actually be saying in their quaint lingo."

"I know the language of whales."

"Oho!" Schubert smiled at Mark. "But of course! You mentioned it before. How can I be surprised at yet another talent you possess? Our submarine hitchhiker here," he winked at the scientist, "knows whale talk. Well then, what are they saying, Mark?"

"They tell me . . . they wish to go home."

"Tut-tut. Nobody here wants to go home, my good young man."

"He is correct, Mr. Schubert," the scientist said without inflection.

"Hunh?"

"Initial analysis of their repeated squeals indicates that message."

"Humph. Balderdash. First hunches are usually incorrect, in science. Tell them to plug in a new diode or something. No whale would say such a thing. Look at them. Did you ever see whales swimming in such satisfied circles?"

They walked back over to the tank and looked in the port.

"Ah, yes. One happy set of orcas. Nice water, even temperature, no pollution, safe and secure environment. They don't even have to hunt for food. We feed them very well. Plankton cubes as you yourself tasted. Even an occasional small turtle, which are the most succulent kind, and a rare delicacy on the open market."

Mark stared into the port, turning his head slightly to put his ear nearer the glass.

Elizabeth stood tensely before the silent, blank monitors, talking on the red telephone. Ernie stood nearby, scanning sheets of transcriptions of conversations during his dive, and the monitored path of Mark's exploration subsequent to it.

"No contact so far, Admiral," she said, her voice raspy and dry. "The S & R unit is making another pass above the trench."

"Your assumption," came the admiral's weary voice, "is that he's trapped on the bottom?"

"Well, 'trapped' is a bit more conclusive a word

than I'm willing to use. I believe he has not left the bottom, and that he is probably still in the general area where we lost him. I have a feeling, sir, if I may."

"You may."

"I have a feeling that he is still viable."

"And on the mission?"

"That I don't know."

"You say you picked up a second dot on your scope."

"Yes. And then they both disappeared."

"Hmm. Do you think it's possible, Dr. Merrill, that the second dot could have been another of his own kind, that he hitched up with?"

"I don't see how, sir. Mark's signal was from the transponder. It would be highly unlikely that somebody else like him was down there with a transponder. The signal we got was electronic."

"I see, yes."

"But I think I must now admit to you, sir, since we have no solid evidence to the contrary, that it's indeed possible that Mark—as you suggested before—just forgot about us and took off."

There was a pause.

"Do you believe that, Doctor?"

"No."

"Then you keep searching."

They stepped into a dark room. Schubert turned a rheostat dial on the wall, and the lights came on gradually, illuminating the room with a dim, dramatic glow.

"This is the rest of my stuff," Schubert said. "My storehouse."

The room was filled with statuary, some still encrusted with coral.

Mark approached a full-figure statue of a Greek sea god holding a trident. The head and body were eroded in places from long immersion in the sea. Mark stared at the face, which seemed to be staring back at him. There was a remarkable resemblance between their strong features, deep-set eyes, and fine classical aquiline noses.

He reached out and touched it, with a hand now turning black. His breath came shorter as he moved his hand over the face, tracing its lines.

"My people tell me," Schubert said, waving his hand around, "that all this is the best sculpture the human race has produced. Nobody has to tell me, of course. It's true that some of this is the best mankind has done. Some of it is not. Most people wouldn't know the difference, but I do. I just don't believe in letting anything go to waste. The ocean is still full of stuff I'm saving from the madness up there. You know what I mean by madness?"

Mark took a couple of breaths. "I . . . learn."

"Perhaps, perhaps. Not many human beings learn anything fast enough. Madness. Wastrels and scoundrels control the earth. They don't know the true value of anything. I do. I surround myself with treasures. My inspiration. And one day, those left will appreciate what comes from the sea."

"Those . . . left?"

"Yes." They walked past more statues and fragments. "For three thousand years, they've destroyed our land, air, and water. The nations of the world have been left in the hands of base idiots and crass clods and insensitive boors, with no more esthetic taste than an amoeba. They have planted the seeds of their own destruction. Now they're going to finish each other off in one last big war."

Mark studied him. Schubert's heavy jowls flushed crimson, his small eyes glowed with passion.

"How do you . . . know this?" Mark asked.

"Well, mainly," a twinkle returned to his eyes, "because I'm going to start it."

They passed through a door under a large light shining with a steady green glow. The room they entered was a vast high-ceilinged expanse, a combination of rough walls hewn out of the rock, and banks of sophisticated machinery that hummed and blinked.

In the center of the room, hanging from the ceiling, was a huge lucite projection map of the world. On the oceans were positioned tiny models of various kinds of military ships—submarines, aircraft carriers, missile cruisers—in different colors. A key at the bottom of the map indicated that these colors matched ownership by the various nations.

Scientists and technicians worked at dozens of posts. Every few moments, one of them would step up to the map with a long rod and shift the position of a ship slightly in one direction or another.

Conversation among the workers was brief and businesslike—as elsewhere in the habitat, no pleasantries were exchanged. Voices were low and monotonous. The work was ceaseless and not marked by excitement.

Schubert led Mark to the middle of the room near the map and gestured around at all the people. "You see, I've studied the human animal—not from books, but close up—and I've come to the conclusion that there's no hope for him but to start all over again. And this time to add courtesy, good manners, esthetic judgment, and a modicum of discipline. A sane man, not diverted by myth or empty emotion, could arrive at no other conclusion. Mankind must start over, this time with the values he has always espoused and never heeded. Don't you agree?"

Mark gazed around at the busy scientists and equipment. He didn't answer.

They began to walk slowly around the room, passing the preoccupied scientists, including the four that Mark had followed in. Those four were scribbling on yellow pads, then tapping on pocket calculators, then scribbling some more.

"Now take these folks," Schubert said, "outstanding scientists, every one. Best in their fields. By best I don't mean just in their scientific know-how, but in their attitudes. They are all disillusioned with life upstairs. Every one hates war. Every one was fed up with what they had to do in their own countries, which was primarily to advance the military machines and capabilities of their nations. Call it defense work or corporate research, it was all the same, all work for war. Chemical companies, automobile companies, oil producers, electronics works—all professed peaceful purposes, but all directed to the war machine. Even the food companies. Did you know there is a mustard preparation one cup of which, when properly spiced, has the destructive force of three thousand tons of TNT?"

The British scientist sat at a control board as if hypnotized, his face devoid of expression, his eyes staring at the board, his fingers working the dials mechanically.

"Like this fine gentleman," Schubert said. "In his former life on that decaying isle—that same isle which spawned your decaying country—he was locked into the development of a particular transistor which could have advanced the human condition but was in fact employed only in missiles. He just wanted a chance to work on pure science—as they all do here. And someday—after this little necessary diversion they are presently involved with—they will.

Schubert patted the scientist on the shoulder, getting no reaction, and they moved on.

"You will notice that all the workers here are wearing the bracelet which you have so far unwisely shunned. My little bracelets make it easy—no stress or strain or searching of souls and so forth. It allows them to concentrate fully on their tasks, without intrusion of unproductive emotions or doubts or fears. In short, these handsome bracelets bring you peace. They would be good for everybody, of course, but it's hardly a practical notion to try to get them on four billion people, right? They will not always be necessary—you notice that I am not wearing one. Once minds are reoriented toward the positive thinking that is the acme of the human brain, the bracelets can be discarded—like training wheels on a kid's bike. My mind is so developed."

Schubert chuckled, and Mark looked at him.

"Don't misunderstand me, dear man. This is not humorous. Just happy excitement. Look at all this." He thrust out his palm in several directions toward the scientific equipment, as if pushing each piece into place against the wall. "Know where I got it? Aha. No, no, I didn't sneak into the world's laboratories and abscond with these marvelous and expensive machines. I am a scavenger, my friend. And so it was with this. These items are what's left of Russian spy ships, CIA aircraft, French super-subs—all manner of the world's military craft that met their fates over the seas and went to the bottom filled to the brim with the most up-to-date hardware. Remember the submarine *Thresher* that sank in the Atlantic with all hands? The B-52 hydrogen bomber that crashed through the ice off Greenland? The Russian cruiser *Menshevik* that sprang a leak in the Sea of Okhotsk? Ho. All carrying millions and millions of dollars' worth of fine electronic gear, lost and useless to the surface dwellers. But not to me. I found it all, fixed it up, and put it back to work, right here. So I'm the original recycle king."

He took Mark's shoulders and slowly turned him around to face the giant map dangling from the ceiling.

"See that? That's not your run-of-the-mill atlas, my dear boy. With this map we're keeping track of every nuclear-missile-carrying ship and submarine in the world. Hundreds of them, carrying thousands of warheads, each one aimed at a preselected target in somebody else's backyard, ready to be fired in case of war. We know their precise location, the exact status of their missiles, just where each is aimed."

Schubert puffed out his chest and spread his arms grandly. "Can you imagine what could be accomplished if one man could get control of all that power for thirty seconds. Huh? Well, my friend, I've done it!"

He brought Mark closer to the map. "Look how many of those ships the warmongers have distributed over our globe. Insane. And they fall all over themselves just trying to keep track of each other. Well, we do that with ease. We here have developed signals that are much more accurate and immediate than they have up there. No simple sonar Ping-Pong. And with a bit more canny rewiring and reprogramming, we reach not only the ships, but within them to the very missile-control systems themselves. If you were a scientist, I could explain it to you. But I'll give you a simplified quickie."

Mark turned to study him, his breath growing hoarse. Schubert, in his proud discourse, seemed oblivious to Mark's growing discomfort.

"You see, we make use of their own technology. We don't even need to have missiles of our own. We use theirs. Their missiles are already targeted—everybody's to shoot at everybody else. Arming them is no big deal. Simple push of some buttons on the ships—zip-zap-zup—and they're armed. What takes time on shipboard is that they have to get permission from higher-ups, and the higher-ups have to get permission from higher-ups. We don't. Nothing to firing them—zip, zap, zup. Everything is ready, up there, for pushing buttons. Now, how do we, down here, get those buttons, up there, pushed? All we do is have our systems designed to override all their systems. Their systems do the rest. Our systems send a signal to their systems, bypassing the human idiots, and the job is done. A-B-C, if you know what you're doing."

At that moment, Mark gave a start. He had been watching a man working at a console. Something about the man drew his attention. When the man turned to the side to read a gauge, Mark recognized him.

It was Commander Hendricks, the man who accompanied Commander Roth on the ill-fated mission of the *Sea Quest*.

". . . And we know what we're doing."

Just then Commander Hendricks leaned forward and moved a lever. A *whoomp* echoed in the room, and a finger of flame shot out briefly, knocking Commander Hendricks backward off his chair and onto the floor. He lay still.

A few heads turned toward Hendricks, then turned back to their work.

Mark started forward, but Schubert held him back with an arm.

"Switch to your backup system, Kumkov," Schubert barked to the Russian scientist. Then he smiled at Mark. "A curable problem, my boy. You see we are prepared for human error."

One scientist climbed slowly down from a ladder where he had been tending a second-level console and approached the fallen man. It was Philip Roth, moving stiffly as if sleepwalking. He knelt unsteadily beside Hendricks.

Two guards with rubber nightsticks came briskly through the door and stomped over toward Roth. Mark brushed aside Schubert's arm and took a couple of steps toward the two commanders. The guards whirled around and swung their clubs, grazing Mark and sending him stumbling back against Schubert. Schubert stepped in front of him as the guards pulled Roth erect and left him standing, though wavering a bit.

"Go back to your station, Philip," Schubert ordered.

Roth, in a daze, advanced closer.

"Philip!"

He continued to plod forward.

Schubert nodded calmly to the two guards, who quickly seized Roth and pummeled him with their clubs and hauled him away.

"No." Mark pushed Schubert away. "No."

Two other guards raced in and pinned Mark's arms. He faced Schubert. "I now understand . . . your world." The two locked eyes. "You are . . . wrong."

Mark tried to pull free from the guards, but he staggered and gasped for breath. One guard swung his right fist a single time into Mark's jaw, and Mark dropped to the floor.

"The human animal," Schubert shook his head sadly, "continues to amaze me."

Throughout all this, the other workers continued to concentrate on their machinery, never once distracted by the violence.

"You see, Mark?" Schubert looked down at his still form, his voice soft and pleasant. "Wouldn't it be better if everyone were like my staff here? Fully at peace?"

Rain pelted the deck of the *Moon River*. Elizabeth and Ernie, in yellow slickers, stood together at the rail and looked out into the night, across the empty surface of the ocean.

"I never felt so useless," Elizabeth said softly. "Never felt so absolutely powerless and inept."

"I lost a guy last year, back near home, not far off Catalina." Ernie wiped water off his eyes with his hand. "My co-diver. I didn't know him well. He seemed to know what he was doing. It wasn't a difficult dive. We were down about one-thirty-five checking out an old tanker hulk that was a menace to navigation, to guide the welders in to cut up the superstructure. Things seemed to be going fine. Then it was time to get back up. I signaled to the guy, and he just looked at me. There was a big old grouper that had been nosing around for a while—you know how curious they are. And suddenly my co-diver just slips out of his airpack and takes his regulator and hands it out to this grouper, like he wanted him to breathe through it, you know?"

He shook his head. "Right away I knew he had the rapture. I grabbed him and tried to shove my regulator in his mouth, share my air while I dragged him up. But he just pushed me away. And all at once he kicked and took off straight down. Went right out of sight. All I could see was his air bubbles coming right pass me. He was breathing, right? Breathing his last breath. I wanted to go down after him. But I was just about out of air. Nothing I could do. Nothing."

He fell silent. They looked out into the rain.

He cleared his throat. "You were asking me what I felt, when Mark took off down from the platform. Well, for a couple of minutes, that's what I felt. Like maybe he had the rapture and was gone and there was nothing I could do. But then in my earphones I heard you say he was okay. If you hadn't said that . . ."

She waited. "What, Ernie?"

"I think maybe I woulda gone after him, this time."

The rain whipped their faces and drowned out the rumble of the shipboard generators.

## chapter 8

Green lights began flashing on the rows of monitors and control boards and reflecting off the Lucite map and model ships. The scientists glanced up at the lights, then fixed their attention on the monitors without emotion.

Schubert's voice boomed over the loudspeaker.

"Fellow scientists. What we have been laboring on for so long is about to come to pass. Exactly fifteen minutes from the time I start the countdown, a signal will be generated from this undersea mountain to every missile-carrying vessel on the world's oceans. That signal will penetrate every electronic defense, override every fail-safe system, and activate the mechanisms that will launch every missile atop the sea toward its prearranged target. Then we will sit back and wait for the mess to clear."

The scientists and technicians sat stiffly on their chairs, showing no reactions.

Schubert went on. "Already our preliminary exploratory signal is probing these shipboard systems throughout the world, confirming all our concepts and calculations. In moments, that signal will be withdrawn, and the way will be cleared for the terminal activating signal that will bring a swift end to all that nationalistic nonsense adrift above us. The holocaust will be the final fire. I mean, it will be a beaut. We're going to shake this planet down to the roots and then we're going to fix it up and get it back to speed again—our way. With fewer, but considerably higher quality, people. Just like yourselves. Think about it now as you go back to your quarters. Go."

The emotionless workers rose stiffly from their seats, turned, and began filing out of the vast room. They stayed separated from each other by about a yard, almost in lock step. The big map past which they paced remained lit, the tiny model ships stuck motionless to their stations like flies on flypaper. None of the departing scientists said a word.

Aboard the newly christened, nuclear-powered American aircraft carrier *Patience*, cruising in the North Atlantic, several officers sat around the table in their club room sipping after-dinner Grand Marnier.

"What do you make of that strange signal we were picking up, Captain?" the lieutenant commander asked.

"Not much to make of it. Not your normal signal. Couldn't trace it. No harm done. Russkies playing with some new electronic toy, trying to figure out how it works."

"What makes you think it was the Russians?" Heads turned toward Lt. Maggie McCurdy, the first woman to serve on board.

"Well, heh-heh," the captain said, cocking his head to look at her, "when you've served out here as long as we have, you get to know the Russkies pretty good.

You'll get used to it. If they're serious we're ready for 'em. They know we got bombers on board. But they don't know we got multiheaded Cruise nukes."

"In any case, Captain," said the lieutenant commander, "the signal disappeared a while ago, as quick as it came, and nothing's been heard since."

"So that's that," the captain said.

Aboard the nuclear-powered Chinese submarine *Yamaha* deep in the Sea of Japan, the radio officer turned to the first mate, who was peering over his shoulder.

"It's gone," he said in a heavy Szechwan accent.

"Very strange indeed," said the mate in the lighter inflections of Hunan.

"It was very faint, and not like sonar."

"Hmm."

"And quite distant, not as if from Japanese waters. And it has been reported to me that there was a brief buzzing in the torpedo room."

"So? Perhaps it is in the nature of our new hydrogen warheads to buzz a bit."

"In any event, I haven't been able to pick it up again. Should I keep looking for it?"

"No, no. We'll wait. If the signal returns quickly, we'll know it was the Americans. They are in such a hurry."

"Do you suppose they know we're here?"

"Probably. But they do not know why."

"Why are we here, sir?"

"Ah, my son, to that there are as many answers as there are junks on the Yangtze—none of them known to us. But if the signal returns bearing threat to us, we are prepared to respond in kind."

* * *

Aboard the guided-missile cruiser *Lev* in the eastern Mediterranean, the Israeli officer of the deck trained his binoculars on shore near Beirut.

"Think it was the Egyptians, sir?" asked the young ensign.

"Who knows? We've got lots of friends and lots of enemies. Our friends are just as interested in penetrating our electronics systems as our enemies are."

"You think it could even have been the Americans?"

"Americans, French, Russians, Syrians, Japanese, Ugandans—the list of possibilities is endless. The signal won't come again."

"Why not?"

"Because whoever sent it would not risk its being traced. Everybody wants to spy on us, but nobody wants us to know they're doing it, friend or foe alike. So they sent a feeble signal and learned nothing. Or they learned everything. It makes no difference. They won't do anything. We won't do anything. Nobody wants the Middle East to explode just now—not while they need the oil."

Schubert sat alone in a small, brightly lit room, in front of the master control panel. "Ah, yes," he said softly, "time is money. And now's the time."

He flipped a small metal cover to his left, exposing a lock. He inserted a key into the lock and turned it.

"And so, my pretties above, I have just withdrawn our preliminary signal. Did your delicate hulls feel the pulse of our initial probe? Did your awesome launch mechanisms sense our first electronic tickle? No matter. It was nothing. We were just saying hello. We were saying hello and how are you. And we have our answer. You are all fine and right at home. Enjoy yourselves, my floating babes of warfare. Your time is almost up. Our next signal will be saying good-bye."

He inserted the key in another lock to his right and turned it. A digital readout appeared in the center of the screen in front of him: "15:00."

Now Schubert took out a large golden key, stuck it into the slot of yet a third covering, this one in the middle of the desk just below the numbers, and opened it. Under it was a large red button.

Schubert held his right index finger a few inches above the red button. For a long moment he stared at the unchanging digital numbers. The full range of emotions flitted across his chubby features: hate, anger, bitterness, sorrow; then softening to passivity; then climbing up the other way to expectation, pleasure, joy, and finally ecstasy.

Eyes wide, nostrils flaring, mouth wide in silent laughter, he brought his finger down on the button.

At that instant, the numbers on the digital sequencer began clicking down: "14:59 . . . 14:58 . . . 14:57 . . ."

The steel shark cage hung suspended by cables just beneath the concrete ceiling, ten feet above the water of the docking channel. Mark lay barely breathing on the floor of the cage, his hands nearly black, his face darkening.

Seated with his back against the close-spaced iron bars, staring blankly, was Lieutenant Commander Roth.

Strong floods lit the cage, the lights burning Mark's skin and baking his eyes. He moved slightly, raised an arm and dropped it. He was still for a moment. Then he rolled painfully onto his side, struggled to lift himself. He pushed himself up on one arm, reaching the other toward Roth.

His hand fell short by a yard. He managed to get both elbows under himself and started to drag his body forward, inch by inch, closer to Roth.

Finally he raised his right arm and reached. His fingers touched Roth's wrist, and gradually encircled it. Like claws, Mark's fingers gripped the bracelet and, with a final surge of energy, ripped it off Roth's wrist.

Mark watched it drop to the floor of the cage.

Roth blinked. He turned his head slowly and looked down at Mark, bewildered, as if waking from a dream.

Footsteps sounded below. Schubert walked out of a corridor onto the walkway beside the channel. "Truly a pity," he called up, "that you boys have to be treated in such a demeaningly appropriate manner. You arrived like men, you will leave like fish."

Mark slid his head to the side of the cage and looked down, his eyes dull.

"Ah, yes, it's a shame. Such potential. So much you could have done and enjoyed. So much you will miss. You'll see nothing of the splendid new order of things. And to think you came *that* close," he held his index fingers an inch apart, "to being a part of it all."

Roth leaned against the bars and looked down at Schubert, blinking and moving his head from side to side as if to loosen the tension in his neck.

"Well, I'm sorry you fellows didn't have the gumption to go the whole way with us. But," he shrugged, "if you can't stand the heat, you have to get out of my kitchen."

His belly quivered from a chuckle. He stepped over to the wall and pushed a button. Two levers popped out of the wall. He pulled one of the levers down.

Hydraulic pumping noises came from within the wall. The cables began to lower the cage.

Schubert watched somberly as the cage dropped slowly toward the water of the channel. When it was within two feet of it, he shrugged a final time, turned, and disappeared into the corridor.

The cage continued to creak downward. Mark reached his blackened hands to the bars and pulled himself over to them. The muscles in his arms and shoulders and chest tensed and rippled with strain as he tried to pull the bars apart. But he hadn't even the strength of a normal man. He fell onto his back, gasping for breath. He turned his head weakly toward Roth. "Help . . . me . . ." he moaned pitifully. "Help me . . . the water . . . must have water."

The cage touched the water. The floor dipped under the surface. Water poured between the bars, washing across the floor. Mark tried to roll over to get his face into it. He rose briefly on one elbow, then fell back, his head whacking against the floor.

He lay still. No more hoarse breathing sounds came from his blackened face.

Roth began to stir. He got down on his hands and knees and crawled over to Mark. He slid his arms under him and tried to roll him over to get his face into the water. He was too weak. He fell to his side. "I'm sorry," he muttered, ". . . sorry."

The cage sank deeper. The water covered Mark. It rose over Roth's hips. Still Mark did not move. Roth's eyes were closed. He leaned against the bars of the cage as the water climbed to his chest.

* * *

Schubert sat staring intensely at the digital countdown: "12:34 . . . 12:33 . . . 12:32 . . ."

"Time flies or drags," he mused to himself, "whichever you don't want it to do."

He leaned back and put a finger alongside his nose. "One wonders, at a time like this, whether one has forgotten anything." He wrinkled up his mouth and nose and eyes in thought. "Nope. Not a single item has escaped my attention. How nice to know one has been so thorough in such a monumental and demanding task!"

He leaned forward again to stare at the numbers: "11:58 . . . 11:57 . . ."

The cage was now almost completely under the water. Roth, paddling feebly, had risen with it. His head now bumped the top of the cage. The water was at his neck. There was no more room.

He coughed and choked as he tried to keep the water out of his mouth. He tilted his head far back and pressed his face against the top of the cage, to allow a few more moments of breath before the water covered him completely.

Suddenly Mark began to move on the floor. He turned slowly and raised his head. His metallic green eyes had renewed luster.

He saw Roth struggling above him. He darted to the top of the cage and clamped Roth firmly in his arms to stop his thrashing, then put his mouth close to Roth's ear. "Listen . . . Breathe."

Roth continued to struggle, gasping wetly as water trickled into his mouth and nose.

"Breathe . . . Trust me . . . Breathe."

Roth's eyes were wild. He took some quick, shallow breaths.

"Deeply . . . You must . . . breathe deeply!"

Roth closed his eyes and drew in one last long breath.

With a sudden powerful lurch, Mark jerked him under the water to the bottom of the cage. Planting his feet firmly on the floor and keeping Roth in front of him, Mark reached around and took the bars in his hands and wrenched them apart, twisting them into an opening just large enough.

He quickly backed through the opening, pulling Roth with him. Clear of the cage, Mark shot for the surface. He broke water and yanked Roth's head clear. Roth gasped and coughed.

Holding Roth in one arm, Mark swung to the side of the channel, hoisted himself up on the concrete walkway, and pulled Roth up after him.

Water poured off their white suits. Mark's skin was lightening.

Roth lay flat on his back, his chest heaving. Mark knelt beside him. He glanced quickly around, then fixed his gaze on Roth. He watched him carefully, sensing the status of his recovery, waiting patiently while Roth pulled mouthfuls of air back into his starving lungs.

Schubert left his master control, walked briskly down the corridor and entered the big room where minutes before so many scientists had been hard at work. Now the room was empty, except for the glowing desk monitors and the huge map which hung, brightly lit, in the center of the room.

The room was eerily quiet. Red lights flashed along

the walls. Sequencers counted silently down: "10:54 . . . 10:53 . . ."

Schubert turned to the map and stared up at the facsimiles of oceans and the hundreds of missile ships of several nations. The sequencer in the map clicked down: "10:48 . . . 10:47 . . ."

He nodded with satisfaction.

"The report on Mark Harris, Mr. Schubert."

Schubert spun to see George, the supervisor, standing in the doorway holding a sheaf of papers.

He waved to George impatiently. "Come on, come on, let's have it. A bit late. What took you so long?"

"Chemical anomalies required rescreening."

"Yes, yes, always something that has to be done over. Gimme it." He snatched the papers from George's hands. "And our friend's special adornment?"

"Adornment?"

"The special bracelet, man, don't be such a dimwit. Must I speak to you like a child?"

"Yes, the bracelet." George reached into his pocket and took out the bracelet. It was thicker than the one he wore, and not of a single, solid color, but striped green, red, and black.

Schubert grabbed it and held it up to the light, smiled pleasantly, and nodded. "Fine. Excellent. By the way, George . . ."

George looked at him dully.

"We're going to be celebrating very shortly." He lowered his voice confidentially, leaning toward the supervisor. "George, there'll be a hot time in the old town tonight."

George gazed ahead stonily.

"All right, all right," Schubert dropped his smile and fluttered his hand, "that's it. You're dismissed."

George turned and plodded out.

"Well now," Schubert sat down in a swivel chair and planted his feet up on a desk, "let's see what we have here." He fingered the special bracelet in one hand while he thumbed through the pages of the report with the other.

"Hmm . . . Aha! . . . Hmm." His face mirrored the discoveries the pages presented. Finally he turned over the last page of the report, and tossed it on the desk and clasped his hands behind his head and stared at the ceiling.

"Hmm. Afraid of something like that. Should have thought of it myself."

Abruptly he sat up, reached to press a button, then leaned toward a microphone on the desk.

"Guards. This is Mr. Schubert. Check the shark cage immediately for two bodies. If you don't find them there, that may mean they're still alive. Scour every water chamber and tunnel in the habitat. You are looking for the gentlemen we know as Roth and Harris. If they are alive, we may have a water-breathing man with us. So treat him with care, understand? The one named Harris, I want him alive!"

He leaned back and looked at the bracelet. "Hmm. Useful after all . . ."

There were splashes in several water tunnels as Schubert's guards, wearing white scuba gear with white air tanks on their backs and white helmets with bright spotlights strapped on them, dove in for the search. Rubber fins fluttering rapidly, they moved off down the tunnels, turning their heads slowly right and left to cast their beams against the walls.

* * *

Mark slipped out of his clean-room suit. He helped Roth sit up and ripped the top part of his suit off him.

Then he squatted beside Roth, who was sagging with exhaustion, his legs dangling out over the water.

"Listen to me . . ." Mark put a hand on his shoulder. "Get the others . . . whoever you can . . . Take the bands from their wrists . . . lead them to the submarine."

Roth shook his head wearily.

"You must . . . Your friend Hendricks . . . others . . . You must find them . . . get them to the submarine." He shook Roth's shoulder.

"No good," Roth mumbled.

"Yes . . ."

"The sea lock," he panted between his words, "the door to the sea. Closed."

"I will open it."

"How can you . . ."

"I can open it . . . Trust me."

Roth let his head sag forward. "But Schubert—his signal beam will set off the missiles." He sucked for breath.

He looked up at the sound of a slight splash, and saw Mark disappear into the water.

"Gotta find the others," he muttered as he struggled to his feet. "Gotta find them . . ." He moved off unsteadily down the corridor, supporting himself against the wall with one hand.

Elizabeth took the phone that Commander Johnson handed her. She took a deep breath as she put it to her mouth. "Yes sir."

"You've found nothing," came the admiral's resigned voice.

"No sir. Nothing. I'm sorry, Admiral . . ."

"No need to tell me that, Dr. Merrill. I know. We all are. Are you ready to abandon the search then?"

"Yes . . . yes . . . we are."

"I'm not ordering you to."

"I understand."

"As far as I'm concerned, this is still your mission. If you wish to continue the probes, I will support you."

"Thank you, sir. But I guess," tears slid down her cheeks and she quickly wiped them away with the back of her hand, "I guess there's no sense in continuing. I've already so informed Commander Johnson."

"It's a tragedy, Doctor, for all of us."

"Yes, it's a great loss. Mark was . . ."

"Not just Mark Harris or the *Sea Quest*. I understand that Commander Roth was a good friend of yours."

"Yes."

"If I didn't tell you before, I'm terribly sorry you've lost your friend."

"Thank you. That's all then?"

"Yes. I'll see you back here. Stay tough."

"I'm okay."

Admiral Pierce hung up the phone quietly, then smashed a fist into the side of the desk.

"Anything I can do, sir?"

"No, Ainsley, thank you. You've shaped up well, supported me all you can. There's nothing you can do."

"I guess I'm learning a little bit about command, sir."

"Yeah." The admiral slumped in his chair and stared out the window. "But it's situations like this you can't really prepare for. You don't know how you're gonna handle yourself. You don't know until you're in the middle of it. Then you learn how good a commander you are."

"If I may say, sir, you've done everything possible, really stuck by your people in the field."

"Yeah. For all the good it did. Everybody did everything they could. Trouble is, we just don't know enough about the bottom of the ocean."

Roth moved cautiously along the tunnel, gradually recovering his strength and bearings. He stopped abruptly when he heard the sound of running feet coming from a side tunnel off to the left.

He looked around frantically for a place to hide. There was none, not even the smallest niche in the smooth concrete walls.

He plastered himself against the wall, waiting.

Two guards emerged from the side tunnel and fortunately turned the other way and continued running.

He waited a moment, then turned down the tunnel from which they had come.

He saw an open door and edged up to it, peeking around the jamb. The small room was empty. On one wall was a digital sequencer ticking down: "10:26 . . . 10:25 . . ."

He slipped past the door and continued on, quickening his pace.

Ten minutes, he thought, ten minutes left in a lifetime.

Mark swam slowly through the dimly lit water tunnel, peering ahead, careful to make no sound or disturb the water more than necessary. His undulating movements allowed him to glide without causing a ripple on the surface.

Suddenly he froze, sensing something. He dove for the bottom and flattened himself against it like a flounder.

Three guards in scuba gear appeared out of the distance ahead of and above him, their lights arcing back and forth from one side to the other. They swam swiftly over him and disappeared behind.

Mark rose and resumed gliding forward.

What he could not know was that the guards that had just swum past had completed their assigned circuit twenty yards further on, and had turned and were retracing their path.

Mark passed the entrance to a side channel on his left and continued forward several yards, until he glimpsed two more light beams approaching him from in front.

He turned and swam back toward the entrance to the side tunnel he had just passed.

But now the first set of guards was already at that entrance. He was caught between Schubert's advancing hunters.

They spotted him, closed on him, lunged for him—two from one side, three from the other.

Mark dove for the bottom, trying to slip under them. Suddenly a net dropped over him. He spun and kicked up one side of it, slipping under the edge. The guards swirled the net, trying to snare him again. He was slippery as an eel, darting around faster than the guards could follow him.

Shooting up suddenly, he grabbed the net and hurled it over their heads, snapped it tight, banging their heads together. Then he sped off down the side channel, flashing under the floodlights that pierced the water.

Roth found the Russian, British, and American scientists seated together in a small room, staring at the sequencer on the wall: "8:15 . . . 8:14 . . ."

He quickly stripped off their bracelets. "Where's Commander Hendricks?" he whispered.

They gazed at him, blinking.

"Hendricks! Where is he?"

They all shook their heads.

"Come on!"

He herded them out into the hallway and shoved them in front of him, moving in the general direction of the submarine dock. They stumbled often. He prodded them more, while mindful of the fact that they were moving as fast as they could, trying to refocus their minds after having the bracelets removed.

Two guards appeared suddenly from a junction of corridors just ahead. The three scientists combined to latch onto one guard. Roth leaped at the other and felled him with a quick karate chop to the side of the neck. Then he similarly dispatched the second one.

The action seemed to speed the scientists' reorientation, and now they moved more quickly toward the sea-lock tunnel.

Mark slipped out of the water, sprang to his feet, and dashed soundlessly on bare feet toward the closed doors of the huge control room.

As he neared them, the doors slid open.

He moved cautiously through them into the cavernous room. He prowled along the banks of panels and control units. They buzzed and hummed and pulsed with signals. Above them on the various sequencers the numbers silently tolled down: "8:10 . . . 8:09 . . ."

He leaned over the control units and ran his hands along the desks, searching for crucial buttons or levers.

"Ah, Mark Harris!"

Mark swung around to see Schubert step from behind the huge map of the oceans.

Schubert was grinning wryly. "Welcome to Control. I've been waiting for you. What took you so long?"

Mark's green eyes burned a path into Schubert's beady brown ones.

Schubert stood grinning, tapping his palms together.

Mark stood with feet apart, his arms tensed at his sides. "Stop the signal beam . . . Open the door to the sea."

"You want the door open?" His voice was gleeful. "Nothing to it. Open it yourself, my lad." He fluttered a hand toward the desks. "Merely depress the lighted button."

Mark whirled around. Up and down the row of desks, all the buttons were lit.

Schubert giggled behind him as he pulled the bracelet from his jacket pocket and polished it on his sleeve. "Confused? Pity. Ah, me. All buttons look the same. And of course, you don't know which of those buttons might override the countdown and prematurely blow all the ships at sea sky-high, and all their nations with them.

Mark turned back toward him.

Schubert chuckled again. "Forgive me. But there's no time for me to give you a course in how this all works. Pity you couldn't have been more cooperative and understanding earlier; then I could have taught you everything. But then, let bygones be bygones. I'm an amicable sort." He moved over to one wall, keeping an eye on Mark. "An affliction of a warped adulthood coupled with my insatiable desire to be friendly—and I do want to be friendly with you—causes me still to wish to get to know you better, once our little upstairs job is done."

He pressed a lever in the wall, and another door opened near the end of the row of monitors. He went quickly over and stepped through, beckoning to Mark. "Come join me, Mark. Let's do be friends."

Mark followed him though, and the door closed behind them. They were in a much smaller room with yet another set of controls.

Schubert extracted the report from his inside pocket, unfolded it, and waved it at Mark. "I liked you when we first met. Does that surprise you? It shouldn't. I admire special strength and intelligence. And now that I've read this report on your innards, telling me what makes you tick, I *really* like you. And I know all about you—where you're strong and where you're weak. Being out of water is to you what his heel was to Achilles, what kryptonite was to Superman."

Schubert smiled and riffled the pages of the report with a thumb. "Ah, had I but known that earlier, when I plunked you into the water in the shark cage. Such a foible of mine, at times to act in haste! In my ignorance, I actually restored your strength! Can you beat that?" Schubert chuckled and shook his head.

Mark took a step toward him.

"Ah-ah-ah," he waggled a finger at Mark, "don't be hasty now. You're a visitor to *my* house, you know.

*My* turf. Here we play by *my* rules. Before you could do a thing, I could put a hole in your head with a laser. I could blind you with a light. I could fry you to a crisp with ultrasonics that in ten seconds would leave you lifeless as a dried fish in the desert."

He stepped quickly to the wall, putting his hand up beside a row of buttons. "See? Each of these controls a real goodie I could use on you. But I don't wish to do that unless you behave as an unworthy guest. And I value you highly as a guest. Because of what's in *here*." He waved the report, directing Mark's attention to it while with his other hand he secretly slipped the bracelet out of his pocket and held it behind his back.

"But not to worry. I never waste anything valuable that comes to me from the ocean."

Schubert stepped over to a small separate bank of controls, central to which was a single prominent lever. "I'm going to trade your friendship for the lives of those lesser people who apparently wish to leave *our* underwater habitat. Yours and mine, lad. See here?" He motioned to the lever.

Mark cocked his head suspiciously. Above the lever were letters clearly identifying it: SEA-LOCK GATE.

"Come on over here," he gave a friendly wave, "and do the honors yourself."

Mark looked back and forth from Schubert to the lever.

"Yes, the door to the sea. The door to freedom for your friends."

Mark took a hesitant step toward the lever.

"Come on, lad, nothing to it."

He moved closer.

"Right this way."

Mark raised his hand and put it on the lever.

Instantly Schubert snapped the bracelet on his other wrist.

At once Mark appeared calm and placid, his eyes dulled.

They looked at each other.

"Just take it easy, now," Schubert said sternly, "and remove your hand from that lever."

Mark slowly pulled back his hand. A sequencer behind him on the wall clicked down to 6:43.

Schubert smiled. "That was the correct switch, you know. I don't lie to my friends. And I know you're going to grow to be my . . ."

While their eyes were locked, Mark had slipped off the bracelet, and now, in a flash of movement, he clamped it on Schubert's wrist. Schubert immediately went quiet, his features drooped.

Mark dropped Schubert's wrist, which dangled limply with the bracelet on it. "The ocean that taught you has also taught me. When it senses danger, the sea animal prepares itself and self-regulates a portion of its body. Someday I will teach you how to do it. Now . . . stop the signal beam."

Schubert stared at him with listless eyes and spoke in a listless voice. "The signal beam cannot be stopped. The countdown sequence is automatic."

Mark scanned all the dials and levers hurriedly. "Can the mountain be filled with water?"

"Yes."

"This room? All the rooms? Everything?"

"Yes."

"Will that stop the beam?"

"I don't know."

"Do it."

Schubert turned to the main console. His movements were deliberate. He took a key from his pocket and turned it in a lock in the face of the console. A small compartment opened. Inside was a row of buttons.

The sequencer ticked off 05:58 when Schubert pushed the first of the series of buttons.

To either side of the sea-lock gate, rows of enormous concrete louvers opened. Sea water gushed in through them. The surface of the water channels throughout the complex began to rise.

In the corridors, water began to pour from all the overhead light fixtures.

Roth and the three scientists stumbled, slid, fell, got back up, struggled against the surge of water in the corridors already four inches deep.

Roth splashed ahead. He made a wrong turn into a deserted office. He had just time to note the wall sequencer clicking past 04:17 before he pushed them all back out and continued down the corridor.

Two guards came slogging toward them. But as the four tensed for the confrontation, the wide-eyed guards just kept moving past, staring straight ahead.

They came to a four-way junction. Roth peered frantically down each one.

The sound of gushing water seemed to be loudest through the tunnel to his right.

Roth guessed that the water would be coming in through the main gate. So they turned and splashed off toward the loudest sound.

In moments they burst through the end of the tunnel into the dock area, lit now with but a single battery-powered flood. They saw the Pacific coursing through the concrete louvers. Ahead of them lay the sub.

The water was up around their hips and flowing against them. They locked hands and strained against the current. Finally they reached the side of the strange, quadri-modular craft that had brought them here. The sub bobbed in the forceful stream.

Roth helped each of the scientists onto the conning tower ladder, and they clambered up and dropped through the hatch.

Roth looked behind him, scanning the corridors urgently for any sign of Mark.

A new torrent of water slammed him against the side of the wallowing sub, washing over his head.

Reflexively he reached for the lowest rung of the ladder, found, it, pulled himself up. He reached the top of the conning tower, slipped down inside, pulled the hatch shut over him, and spun the lock-wheel to seal it.

He dropped to the bridge deck and raced forward to the controls. He pulled levers, pushed buttons, and brought the sub to life.

The sub began to submerge. The engines hummed beneath them. They felt the first slight forward thrust from the propellers.

Roth jabbed at two buttons near the helm. The powerful headlights came on.

Suddenly Roth's shoulders slumped. He turned off the engine and slowly turned to face the expectant scientists huddled behind him.

He shook his head. "It's no good. The gate is closed. There's no way out of here."

They all stared out the forward ports at the massive gate.

Red lights pulsed over the console. From deep within the complex, a siren wailed. The sequencer counted inexorably down: "05:02 . . . 05:01 . . . 05:00 . . . " The first drips of water trickled down the wall.

Mark watched the gauges that indicated that flooding had commenced. He turned to Schubert. "Now open the door to the sea."

Schubert reached mechanically for the lever he had teased Mark with before, and pulled it down. The red light above it continued to flash.

Schubert looked at the red light. "The sea-lock control is not functioning."

"It must!" Mark grabbed his shoulder and swung him around. "Why?"

"Perhaps the moisture now dampening the walls is responsible for deadening the terminals."

Mark leaped toward the lever and swung his fist, smacking the concrete beside it, mashing it inward.

The red light above it stopped flashing. Then an adjoining green light blipped on, sputtered, and finally glowed steadily.

"The connections have been made," Schubert droned. "The sea-lock gate is opening."

In the sub, they saw with disbelief that the gate was magically lifting.

Roth jumped back to the controls. Headlights came back on; engines hummed at an increasing pitch; the propellers began to push the sub forward toward the yawning gate.

A cheer went up from the scientists.

"Mark Harris got us out," Roth said grimly, bringing a halt to their cheers.

"Who?" one of them asked.

"A friend. He's still in there."

The scientists looked back, as if they could see into the habitat. They became quiet and backed away from Roth, watching him as he steered the sub toward the row of lights outside the gate.

Just as the sub cleared the gate, all the homing lights in the dock and outside went off.

Roth closed his eyes for a few moments. The sub was silent except for the humming of the engines.

Then he opened his eyes and stared out into the gloom where the headlights lit a path between the canyon walls.

He guided the sub into the Mariana Trench, one hand on the helm, the other working the levers on the flotation panel, causing the sub to rise evenly away from the ocean floor as it proceeded ahead.

Mark pulled Schubert out of the small chamber into the huge control center. Water slid in streams from several cracks in the walls and cascaded over control panels.

In the center of the room, water spilled over the giant map, flooding down over the plastic oceans, dislodging the miniature ships and sending them splashing onto the floor where they floated around as if they'd come to life.

The digital sequencers alone seemed undisturbed: "04:29 . . . 04:28 . . . 04:27 . . ."

Mark picked up Schubert's wrist and snapped off the bracelet and let it fall into the swirling water at their ankles.

Sirens continued to wail in the distance.

Mark looked deep into Schubert's blinking eyes. "I am sorry . . . for all of this . . . I have no anger."

Then he turned and trotted off through the main door and out into the corridor.

The water deepened quickly along the concrete walkway. Mark plodded through it. Two guards splashed desperately toward him just ahead of a new wave.

Suddenly they were inundated, and they tumbled past Mark, their arms and legs flailing under the water.

Mark started to reach for them when a series of explosions wracked the big room just behind him, sending chunks of concrete slamming into the wall around his head and causing a surge of water to hurl him away.

Mark allowed himself to be carried some distance in the surge, then began swimming through one corridor after another where a half hour before scientists had walked in dryness.

Pieces of electronic equipment and furniture drifted past him. Scientific books, their pages flowing in the tide, fluttered past like seabirds.

He swam down the final corridor toward the sea lock. Below him on the submerged floor, heads and torsos and feet and arms of smashed statues tumbled and bounced in the mighty current.

Mark moved steadily against the full force of the tide, heading toward the biggest source of the water—the sea-lock gate.

Then he was at the dock. The single floodlight high in the corner of the ceiling bathed the area in an eerie glow.

The sub was gone. Water coursed through the louvers and the gate.

He started to move off toward it.

"Mark, my boy!"

Schubert's voice came over the loudspeaker, filtering down into the water. Mark stopped. He surfaced quickly. He saw one ceiling camera slowly turn toward him.

"Yes, Mark, I can see you. Strange as it may seem, one monitor is still working. I made ample preparations, you see, so that in the event that all other scanning systems failed, I would still have my own private one . . ."

Schubert sat at his desk before his monitor, water lapping up around his legs. His mouth was twisted into a strange smile. On the screen, he saw Mark looking up into the lens, only his head visible above the rolling water in the sea lock.

"A valiant effort, my boy, but nonetheless merely an effort. Like so much of mankind's vain acts, there is a nobility in the effort, though the attempt may fail. Pity. The only nobility should be in success. Success is mine. Just ten seconds now."

He watched the digital sequencer above the monitor. ". . . 00:08 . . . 00:06 . . ."

Then the monitor showed an explosion in the dock area. Schubert saw an eruption of debris, and saw Mark hurled across the water.

"A water-breathing man. What a loss. Just three seconds . . ."

But then the sequencer stopped, frozen on "00:03."

"No!" Schubert rose from his chair. "It's not poss—"

One final explosion shook the entire habitat.

* * *

Mark's left side was numbed by the first explosion that shattered the dock.

He pulled himself toward the gate, using only his right arm. Something in the gate mechanism seemed to have been broken loose by the blast, and the gate began sliding unevenly down.

He dove toward the diminishing opening, pulling furiously with his good arm in a sidestroke he had never used before.

He was just a few feet away, the gate lowering to just above his head, when the final explosion blasted him forward unconscious.

# chapter 9

Elizabeth leaned over the rail staring with unfathomable sadness across the sea in which odd bits of debris floated. The seismographs had recorded a series of explosions on the ocean floor—too brief and narrow in scope to be an earthquake or volcano, but enough to toss the U.S.S. *Moon River* for several hours.

No one had an explanation for the explosions. But to Elizabeth they meant that whatever slender hope she might have had for Mark's return had been annihilated in the horrendous blasts seven miles down.

While technicians within the ship puzzled over the data recorded from the explosions, tears rolled down Elizabeth's cheeks. Whatever had happened beneath the sea might dazzle, amuse, and occupy the world's marine scientists for years. But it was of no interest to her. No scientific matter at all could tempt her.

It was as if all she had lived and worked for had been blown apart in those mighty, mysterious eruptions so far down below.

Ernie came up behind her, hesitated, then gently touched her shoulder. She turned to him. He pulled her close and wrapped his arms around her.

She buried her face in his shoulder and lost herself in quiet weeping.

The ship churned through the sea toward the coast of California. It was quiet aboard. Scientific personnel were closeted with their several private thoughts. The crew went about its routine duties with somber professionalism.

Elizabeth and Ernie leaned their elbows on the rail and stared out over the sea. Behind them, as bells tolled 1500 hours, the deck watch headed for the stern, strolling casually past the empty diving well.

Had he looked into the well he would have seen that it was not empty. A hand was sliding up the inside wall toward the top edge. Fingers clasped the edge, slipped off, regained it, and held. Then another hand appeared, scratching up the side, reaching the edge. It too held. For several minutes this unseen pair of hands gripped the edge of the diving well. There was no movement, no sound.

Elizabeth fought to keep all thoughts out of her mind, to keep her brain a blank. She strained instead to listen for the sounds of the home-bound ship—the faint creakings of the hull, the footsteps of the working crew, the rustling of a line slithering across the deck, the deep rumble of the engines.

Suddenly she and Ernie both heard another sound: a low moan coming from the diving well.

Ernie sprinted over, dropped to his knees, and reached down to haul Mark up onto the deck. For a moment he lay there, then he struggled to his feet.

Elizabeth stood speechless, gaping, too stunned to speak or go over to him.

Mark staggered slightly, and Ernie supported him.

"I must report . . ." Mark said weakly, "that I did not find the *Sea Quest* . . . But I found Commanders Roth and Hendricks . . . I do not know if they are . . . alive or dead."

He sank against Ernie's arms, but ignored his pleading to lie down.

Now Elizabeth dashed over and threw her arms around him, hugging him tightly. Then she released him and stepped back. She thought she had already used all her tears, but more flooded her eyes now. "Mark . . . Mark, you're all right . . ."

"There is something wrong . . . with your eyes."

"No . . ." She quickly wiped her tears away—though more immediately took their place. "Nothing's wrong. I don't understand how you . . ."

"There is much . . . I must tell . . . Perhaps we should go to your office . . . where you have recording equipment."

"Later, Mark, later. First you must—"

"No. I must tell you everything . . . now. Then . . . I can rest."

Before they had arrived at port, word had preceded them that the strange submarine had already docked, and that Commander Roth and the others seemed in good health, though dangerously exhausted. All had been hospitalized for rest.

Now Elizabeth and Mark sat in the black armchairs facing a relieved and proud Admiral Pierce. Elizabeth was wearing a civilian pantsuit, Mark was clad in Navy dress blues.

"What I'm trying to say, Mark," the admiral was

saying, "is that the good people in this world have to stick together." He made a little temple with his hands. "What do you think about that?"

"I think you are right."

"Well, then," the admiral smiled and nodded, "you've decided to accept my offer."

"Admiral, you are a good man. I have met many good people in your world. But I cannot know your world as you do. You cannot know my world as I do. Let us each stay in our own worlds." He rose from his chair.

"Sorry, Mark," the admiral shook his head, "but it's too late for that. We're already in your world. We are becoming more involved with it every day. Human curiosity and thirst for knowledge will persist. You could help us go into your world in the right way."

"You don't need me. You have your machines."

"Machines aren't going to be able to do what you can do for a long time, Mark, if ever. And right now there are a lot of problems to solve—medical, scientific, defense . . ."

Elizabeth had been watching Mark closely. Now she glanced at the admiral.

"Also some less-than-friendly people out there. You helped us get rid of one—your Mr. Schubert. There are others."

The admiral studied Mark's face. "He is dead, isn't he?"

"I did not see him die."

"Wasn't he trapped when the undersea mountain exploded?"

"I do not know. I was not trapped."

"Then you think he may be alive?" The admiral's face flushed with dismay.

"I do not know. I do not make guesses. I did not see him die. Let us say good-bye now."

Mark turned to look at Elizabeth, then started for the door.

"We don't have to let you go, you know."

Mark turned back to face him. "I know. But you are a good man. I believe your word."

"Yes. Okay. I wouldn't force you to stay. Thank you for what you've done for us, Mark."

Elizabeth started out of her chair.

"No." Mark held up a hand. "It is best if we say our good-byes quickly. Thank you, Dr. Merrill, for teaching me . . . so much."

He walked out of the door.

Ernie was waiting for him at the bottom of the steps. He stuck out his hand. "Been waiting to congratulate you, Mark."

"Thank you, Ernie." Mark shook hands with him.

"Sometimes I don't know what to think about you." Ernie glanced shyly at the ground. "But one thing I think is that you're one in a million."

"Thank you, Ernie. I am leaving now."

"Where to?"

"Out . . . to the Pacific."

"Sea duty, hunh?" Ernie shuffled his feet awkwardly. "Sure gonna miss you and the razz. Well," he gave Mark a wave, "keep your ears clean."

"Yes." Mark looked away toward the sun dipping beneath the horizon over the Pacific, and moved off toward it.

Elizabeth came running down the steps. "Mark! Mark!"

He stopped and turned back toward her.

She ran up, then stopped and looked into his eyes.

"Mark, please let me be with you when you leave—in the water. Let me say good-bye there."

"Yes. To you only I would like to say good-bye . . . at the water."

The sky had darkened by the time they reached the very beach where Mark had been found. It seemed to Elizabeth that eons had passed since then.

Her beige pantsuit fluttered in the wind as she watched the waves crest and run onto the shore, reaching just to her bare toes before receding.

Mark had stripped off his uniform and now, standing straight and formally in his tight swim trunks, he handed the uniform to her, folded neatly as a flag.

"Mark . . ."

"Again there is something wrong with your eyes."

She looked quickly away. "No . . . nothing . . . just emotions. Feelings."

He cocked his head. "Explain feelings."

"I don't know if I can."

"Water from your eyes again. Explain. I will understand."

"Well," she looked out over the sea, her arms cradling the uniform across her chest, "when you get attached to someone and you're close, you feel happy. But then when they go away, you feel sad. And sometimes you cry. That is the water from your eyes. I was crying. But you don't cry."

"No." Mark shook his head. "I have something to say to you now—and I shall call you Elizabeth." They looked at each other. "Keep your ears clean, Elizabeth."

She smiled quizzically, then in spite of her emotions moments before, began to laugh. "Who taught you to say that?"

"Is it not a custom among divers when taking leave?"

"I guess so." Her eyes moistened even as she smiled.

Mark reached out, lightly touched a tear on her cheek, and brought his finger to his mouth. "It tastes of salt."

She nodded.

"Perhaps we are not so different . . . in some ways."

He turned abruptly and walked into the dark surf. Water splashed up on him. Moonlight glistened off his wet shoulders.

He stopped and turned. "I will remember you."

"Mark . . ."

But he slipped beneath the waves and was gone.

From time to time she could discern his shape moving at the surface of the swells, growing smaller.

"Mark . . ." she said softly.

She continued to stare out across the surf and farther over the limitless Pacific. The tide was moving in and the lips of the waves now curled around her ankles, darkening the cuffs of her suit.

At first she thought what she saw was a piece of debris, riding slowly closer on the waves.

Then, nearer the shore, it rose out of the water and stood erect.

Mark strode toward her. He emerged from the surf and splashed in through the fringe of the waves until he stood before her.

For a long moment they just looked at each other.

"You came back."

"Yes, Elizabeth. I have not yet . . . learned enough."

She smiled and blinked back her tears. She held out her hand.

He took it and held it, as he had in the beginning, when she brought him back to life.